T0328871

The Lying Game

Jennifer Baker

AN ARCHWAY PAPERBACK

Published by POCKET BOOKS

New York   London   Toronto   Sydney   Tokyo   Singapore

AN ARCHWAY PAPERBACK *Original*

An Archway Paperback published by
POCKET BOOKS, a division of Simon & Schuster Inc.
1230 Avenue of the Americas, New York, NY 10020

Produced by Daniel Weiss Associates, Inc., New York

ISBN: 978-1-4814-2878-1

First Archway Paperback printing January 1996

10 9 8 7 6 5 4 3 2 1

AN ARCHWAY PAPERBACK and colophon are registered trademarks of Simon & Schuster Inc.

Printed in the U.S.A.

IL 7+

Secrets can hurt....

Katia—What she doesn't know about boyfriend John Badillo will definitely hurt her.

Keith—If he actually throws the season opener, he'll be a major outcast.

Deb—Sweet sixteen and never been kissed. Deb's social life improves when a tall blond hunk helps her find her birth parents.

Suzanne—Nikki has declared war on Suzanne. May the best woman win!

One

"Charge!" Katia Stein yelled, her tiny frame quivering with excitement. All around her was a confusion of color and sound. The first official football game of the Hillcrest High season was about to begin. Katia scanned the action on the field from where she stood in the jam-packed stands.

"Go, John!" she added, waving and trying to catch the eye of her quarterback boyfriend, John Badillo.

"It's a good thing Katia's on crutches," Victoria Hill said to her best friend, Nikki Stewart, "or she'd probably be standing in her seat." Victoria rolled her eyes in a way that made it clear how much the whole scene bored her. "Young love," she drawled sarcastically. "Isn't it adorable?"

"You're just jealous," Deb Johnson told her from her place on Victoria's right.

"Of Katia? And John?" Victoria asked incredulously. "Please!"

Somewhere in the back of her mind, Katia heard them talking about her, but she didn't care. Her entire attention was focused on the game. To be only a sophomore and dating a senior—let alone the star quarterback—was a dream she'd barely dared believe would come true. But it had. She and John were more in love every day.

"Oh, no," Nikki said suddenly. "I swear, she's everywhere I go. There's no escaping that girl!"

Katia turned her attention from the field long enough to see Suzanne Willis making her way in their direction.

"I hope she's not stupid enough to come over here," Victoria said, putting on her dark sunglasses.

"She's not stupid at all," Deb said. "Why don't you give her a chance?"

Nikki shook her head so decisively that her blond hair was tossed behind her. "No way," she said. "She's had plenty of chances. As far as I'm concerned, I never want to talk to her again." She glared in Suzanne's direction.

Suzanne hesitated for only a second and then turned to the right and walked farther up the bleachers.

"Good!" Victoria said emphatically. "Way to go, Nikki!"

"But Suzanne hasn't *done* anything," Deb commented.

"What are you guys talking about?" Katia finally interrupted, confused. She leaned forward so she could see Nikki, who was on the other side of Deb and Victoria. "I thought you liked Suzanne, Nikki."

2

"Not anymore," Nikki said grimly, throwing an evil look up the stands.

"But she saved your life!" Katia protested. The whole situation was bizarre. The last thing that Katia could remember before the car accident that had almost killed her was being at the huge party Nikki had thrown in Suzanne's honor. Ever since she had regained consciousness, Katia had sensed that her friends were babying her a little, but she hadn't realized they were keeping things from her, too. Obviously a lot had happened while she'd been in that coma.

"I don't get it," Katia persisted, reluctantly abandoning any hope of watching the kickoff. "Did you two have a fight?"

"I don't know if you could call it a fight," Nikki said. "I'm just sick of her, that's all."

"Little Miss I'm-so-cool-because-I-grew-up-in-New-York can't keep her eyes off other people's boyfriends," Victoria volunteered.

Katia gasped. "Did you catch her with Luke again?"

Of course, Victoria had told her all about the time that Nikki had stumbled onto Luke and Suzanne kissing at the golf course. In fact, it was pretty general knowledge now. But they had both apologized, and ever since then Luke and Suzanne had even seemed to be avoiding each other. At least, that was what Katia remembered.

"Nikki isn't going to give Suzanne the chance to get that close to Luke again," Victoria said.

"Wow. I can't believe it," Katia said, sinking into a seat. Suddenly her broken leg was killing her, and the place where she'd had stitches in her right

3

shoulder throbbed painfully. She'd only gotten her arm out of the sling the day before, and she would be in the cast a few more weeks, but she'd stubbornly insisted on going to the game anyway. Deb took Katia's crutches from her unresisting hands and laid them across both of their laps.

"You'd better believe it," Victoria advised. "If I were you, I wouldn't leave Suzanne alone with John for a second."

"But that's old news!" Katia protested. "They only went out a few times, and it was a disaster. John's not interested in her." Even as she said it, though, she felt something go cold in the pit of her stomach. Katia was used to people warning her about John and his terrible reputation for hurting every girl he ever went out with, but coming from Victoria it carried more weight. After all, John and Victoria had dated for a pretty long time.

"John cares about me," Katia added. But it sounded weak, even to her.

Victoria lowered her sunglasses just enough to turn those startling green eyes in Katia's direction and fix her with the type of patronizing look usually reserved for three-year-olds. "Uh-huh," she said.

Suddenly the game was all but ruined for Katia. She knew she should trust John, but she trusted Victoria, too. No one knew John like Victoria. And if Victoria hadn't been able to keep him faithful—beautiful, redheaded Victoria—what chance did Katia have?

"Don't listen to her," Deb whispered, turning her back to Victoria. "You know how Victoria is.

She can't find a boyfriend for herself, so everyone has to suffer."

Katia smiled. Deb was always so nice and down-to-earth. She and Victoria were complete opposites.

"You really think that's it?" Katia asked hopefully.

"I *know* that's it," Deb assured her. "Ever since Ian Houghton totally ignored her on what was supposed to be their big date, Queen Victoria hasn't been herself. Or maybe she's been more herself than usual, if you know what I mean." Deb smiled mischievously as she pulled the brim of her blue baseball cap down lower over her friendly chocolate brown eyes.

"Yeah, I think I do," Katia giggled, feeling better. She felt a little disloyal talking about Victoria like that, but she had to admit that Deb had a point. Victoria could be a true friend, but she could also be a royal pain. And John really did care for Katia—she knew he did. It was dumb to worry.

"So cheer up!" Deb encouraged her. "Look, your boyfriend is about to throw the football."

Luke Martinson's hands were shaking as he stocked CDs at the Tunesmith. His boss, Rick, had walked out of the back room just as Luke was pocketing the two twenties he'd hidden under the register drawer. Luke was sure that Rick hadn't seen him take the money, but he still couldn't stop being nervous.

Stealing from Rick made him almost physically sick. He had promised himself repeatedly that he'd never do it again, but now he was completely broke and just as desperate. If only Mom would get off her butt long enough to keep a job, I wouldn't have to do this, he told himself, but he knew that was only half the truth.

It was true that his mother wasn't carrying her share of the load, that he'd resorted to stealing in order to pay the rent and put a few groceries on the table, but it was also true that he hadn't tried anything else. He could have borrowed from Nikki or one of his other friends—they all had plenty of money—but he was too proud to do it. It was bad enough that he lived in a dirty, cheap apartment and had to spend every spare minute working at the record store just to keep things together . . . that he had to be a parent to his parent. It wasn't fair that he had to beg for money, too. Sometimes it felt as though pride was all he had left.

But he wasn't proud of this. In fact, he'd never been so ashamed of anything in his life.

"Hey, Luke."

Luke practically jumped out of his worn jeans. Rick had come right up behind him—there was no one else in the store.

"Uh, yeah, Rick?"

"I need to talk to you," Rick said, leaning up against the racks. "I just don't know what to do."

"About what?" Luke could feel his hands begin to sweat, and he rubbed his palms nervously against his faded jeans. He knew what Rick wanted to talk about.

"This stealing thing. It's really got me down."

"It's bad news," Luke agreed, feeling like the biggest hypocrite in the world.

6

"No one has come forward, and I know it's someone on the staff. If no one confesses, I'm going to have to fire everyone on Monday."

Luke gasped. He'd never believed Rick would really go through with it. Everyone at the store was going to lose their job, and it was all his fault.

"Don't worry," Rick said, patting Luke on the shoulder. "I know things are rough for you right now and you probably can't afford to be out of work, so I'm going to keep you on. You're the only one I'm keeping."

"Rick," Luke said, overcome with guilt, "I don't deserve this."

"Of course you do!" Rick said earnestly. "You're the best, most dedicated employee I've ever had. I hate having to fire the others, but I couldn't get along without you, Luke."

"But it's not right," Luke said, feeling miserable.

"Believe me, I know that," Rick said sadly. "Five people out of work and only one of them guilty—it tears me up. But don't you worry about it, Luke. It's not *your* fault."

And that's when Luke knew it was over. If he ever wanted to be able to respect himself again, he was going to have to tell Rick the truth—that day.

"Ouch! That must have hurt," Nikki observed as John Badillo went down under a sea of opposing players. "Why didn't he throw the ball?"

"No one was open," Katia defended her boyfriend loyally.

Nikki raised an eyebrow. There must have been

at least three guys John could have thrown to, including Katia's big brother, Keith. Still, it was early—maybe the team just needed to warm up.

At least Suzanne was keeping her distance. Nikki looked up to where Suzanne was sitting alone near the top of the bleachers. She looked so sad and lonely up there that for a moment Nikki almost felt sorry for her. After all, she and Suzanne had had some good times, too. If only Suzanne could have kept her eyes off Luke! But the way Suzanne had acted at the *West Side Story* auditions, singing that love song right to him, practically sitting in Luke's lap afterward . . .

Deb stepped across Victoria to reach Nikki's side.

"Do you want me to ask her to come sit with us?" Deb asked, nodding up the bleachers toward Suzanne.

"No!" Nikki protested quickly. "Of course not."

"Look, Nikki," Deb said, "this may not be my business, but it isn't like you to act this way."

It was true, Nikki acknowledged to herself. She hated the way she was behaving. Despite what some people thought, everything in life didn't always go her way, but she usually handled things better than this.

"I don't know, Deb. There's something about Suzanne. She really gets under my skin."

"I think she just wants to be your friend," Deb said. "She likes you."

"I'm not sure if she *likes* me or she wants to *be* me," Nikki replied, pushing her long blond hair behind her ear. "You have no idea what it's like to have someone

8

move in on your life that way. She acts as though she's practically in love with my father, and now he's paying more attention to her than he does to me!"

"Maybe you're imagining—" Deb began.

"And then there's Luke," Nikki cut in. "She says she isn't after him, but I know she is. I just don't trust her, Deb."

Nikki cast one last look back up the stands, then turned around and faced the field. If she wasn't acting like herself, then it was Suzanne's fault. The sooner she forgot about Suzanne Willis, the better.

"Amen to that," Victoria chimed in, eavesdropping as usual. "If you'll remember, Nikki, I warned you about her right from the beginning."

"I remember," Nikki acknowledged. Boy, did she remember. If only she'd listened!

"I just think the whole thing is getting blown out of proportion," Deb insisted. "She's been great to me. She's really helped me with all this stuff about finding my birth parents. And it couldn't have been easy for her, either, what with just hearing that her own father is alive and not even knowing who he is!"

Nikki saw a familiar sly smile light up Victoria's pale complexion, and Nikki knew what she was thinking. It was Victoria who had unearthed that particular bit of news and revealed it to Suzanne.

"And how much closer *are* you to finding your birth parents?" Victoria pointed out. "I mean, after all of Suzanne's great help."

"What do you want her to do?" Deb countered. "Break into the hospital and steal the birth records? Maybe break into their computer?"

"Now, there's an idea!" Nikki exclaimed. Why hadn't it occurred to her before? "Ian Houghton is practically a computer genius. I'll bet he could get into any hospital's records in about five minutes flat."

"You're probably right," Deb said, a strange expression crossing her face.

Victoria laughed derisively. "Yeah, that's if you can get him to *talk* to you first. I mean, if he wasn't interested in *me* . . . ," she said, alluding to her one disastrous date with Ian. Victoria shrugged in a way that made the rest of her meaning clear. "Let's face it—why bother?"

Deb bristled.

"Look at those two argue," Katia broke in, changing the subject. She pointed to Keith and John, who were standing together on the sidelines, a short distance away from the rest of the team. "They've been acting like idiots all week."

The two friends, with their helmets off, were talking and gesturing furiously, but every couple of seconds one of them would look toward the rest of the team, as if afraid of being overheard.

"What in the world are they doing?" Nikki asked.

"Beats me," Katia said. "They've been fighting all week, but they won't tell me why. Something's definitely up."

The two boys suddenly put their helmets back on and ran to join the rest of the team, slapping each other's butt on the way.

"Guys!" Katia said in mock disgust.

"Speaking of which," Victoria said, turning to Nikki, "where's Luke?"

"Oh, he's coming straight from work," Nikki answered, trying hard not to let her voice give away that he was already very late. "He should be here any second." *If he knows what's good for him,* she added to herself.

Luke paced blindly, frantically, in Rick's tiny office.

"I always meant to pay you back," he said, desperate. "I would have paid you somehow. If there's any way I can—if I can work for free—anything. I just didn't know what else to do. My mom . . ." Luke had to stop. His throat was so tight he could barely speak.

"Luke, this is serious stuff," Rick said from behind his desk. "You've committed a crime. I could have you arrested."

"I know. Please give me another chance," Luke begged.

"How can I ever trust you again?" Rick asked. "And after everything I did for you! Giving you a raise—"

"Please," Luke interrupted before Rick could go on. Every one of his words cut like a knife. "I can't offer you anything except my word, but I'm swearing to you now—nothing like this will ever happen again. Please. If you fire me for stealing, you might as well have me arrested—I'll never get another job in Hillcrest."

"That's probably true," Rick agreed.

"Please, Rick. I was desperate. I would've paid you back."

Luke's heart pounded painfully as he watched

Rick's face. He honestly didn't know if he even deserved a second chance—he just knew he had to have one. Rick leaned back in his office chair and fiddled with a mechanical pencil. Please, God, Luke prayed silently, help me out just this once and I'll never steal anything again.

"Well, it did take guts to tell me the truth," Rick said at last. "Especially when you could have kept your mouth shut and let me believe I'd fired the thief. I guess that counts for something."

"Thank you!" Luke exploded with relief.

"Not so fast," Rick said. "You still owe me some money. I'm not even sure how much."

"I'm pretty sure," Luke said. He fished a slip of brown paper out of the front pocket of his jeans and put it on Rick's desk with a shaking hand.

"I already gave you back what I took today. That's the rest of it," he said, gesturing toward the paper.

Rick stared at the penciled figures with surprise. "Wow! That's quite a chunk of change, Luke. Even more than I suspected."

"I wanted to be sure to pay you back, so last night I wrote down all the times I could remember and then I added a hundred dollars more, kind of like a penalty. I swear that's got to be every penny," Luke admitted.

"Somehow, I believe it is," Rick said, smiling a little for the first time since Luke had spilled his awful secret. "Well, you won't be taking home any paychecks for a while," he added. "I want to see you here bright and early for every shift until this 'loan' is paid off."

"You will!" Luke assured him.

12

"Good," Rick said. "When we're all square, I'll start paying you again. Now why don't you take off? I'll see you tomorrow."

Luke grabbed his black leather jacket and stepped out of the Tunesmith in a daze, barely noticing that the warm afternoon had become cuttingly, persistently chilly. He knew he was late for the football game, at which he'd promised to meet Nikki, and he started walking in that direction automatically, even though football was just about the last thing on his mind.

The relief and gratitude he'd felt when Rick decided not to turn him in to the police had been overwhelming, but now reality was setting in. He wasn't going to jail, but he was still flat broke and couldn't pay the rent. His mom was still a pathetic alcoholic without a job. And now he was going to be working every day for free. How much longer could he keep this up?

Two

Suzanne couldn't remember when she'd ever been so miserable. She hadn't wanted to move to Connecticut in the first place, and now everyone in Hillcrest hated her. Everyone except Luke, and he was off-limits. She looked down the bleachers to where Nikki was sitting with Victoria, Deb, and Katia. She had wanted so badly to be best friends with Nikki, to tell her they were sisters. And this was the thanks she got—Nikki freaking out for practically no reason and then refusing even to speak to her.

If that's the way she wants it, then fine! Suzanne told herself unhappily, looking down on Nikki's group of friends. Nikki and Victoria were dressed like blond and redheaded twins in jeans and T-shirts with leather jackets, but, as usual, Victoria was displaying a little independence in the form of red cowboy boots. It didn't surprise Suzanne a bit that Victoria would go along with Nikki, and she barely knew Katia. But she really thought Deb would have stuck up for her.

Just then a huge groan erupted from the crowd. Keith Stein had fumbled another ball.

"Hey, Stein, you stink!" yelled the guy sitting near Suzanne. He turned toward her slightly to see if she was impressed. He'd been leering at her all afternoon, and Suzanne knew his type too well—he was exactly the kind of loser to assume that any pretty girl sitting alone would rather be with him. She turned her head away, letting her long brown hair shield her from his stare.

Of course, it was true that Keith was having a really bad game. For that matter, her old fling John Badillo wasn't playing so hot, either. It was amazing; everyone had said that Hillcrest was going to win this game against Walnut Hills without even breaking a sweat, but they were already down two touchdowns, and it wasn't even halftime yet.

Suddenly Suzanne didn't know why she'd come. Any illusions she'd had about smoothing things over with Nikki had been totally shattered the second she saw the poisonous way Nikki looked at her. There was no way she could walk over and try to sit with Nikki's group after that. And now their team was losing. Badly. She stood up and began to head down the bleachers.

"Hey! You're not leaving now, are you?" the pest from the next seat bellowed after her.

Suzanne kept walking without looking back and without looking at Nikki. All she wanted to do was get out of there—away from everyone. She'd left her mountain bike chained to the parking lot fence. Maybe she'd take a ride out to Pequot State Park; maybe the fresh air and quiet would help clear her head.

She had just knelt to open the bike lock when she saw Luke Martinson coming across the parking lot. Luke. Her heart still turned over every time she saw him. That night on the golf course, when he'd kissed her and said he had feelings for her . . . Suzanne had thought that everything was going to turn out so differently. But now he was back with Nikki, and Suzanne had to let him go.

Or did she?

All at once she was filled with an angry resolve. I'm not a doormat, she told herself, and I've had just about enough of Nikki Stewart. If she wants a fight, she's going to get one. Starting with Luke!

"Hey, Luke!" she yelled, standing up again and waving in his direction. "Luke! Over here!"

"Don't even talk to me. You make me sick," John hissed. He turned his back on Keith and slid farther down the hard wooden bench.

It had been the worst tongue-lashing from Coach Kostro that Keith had ever heard, and now the team was supposed to sit and think about what he'd said for the rest of halftime. But Keith couldn't concentrate on anything but himself. He had to know if John was going to see this thing through. If John didn't help him throw the game, Keith would never be able to pay back his gambling debts, and if he didn't . . . well, he didn't even want to think about it.

16

"Oh, yeah, like you're so innocent," Keith whispered at John. "And how about keeping your voice down?" He quickly looked around the locker room to make sure none of the other players was listening. "Maybe if you could have controlled yourself enough not to cheat on my sister while she was in a coma, you wouldn't be in this mess right now."

"Don't you dare talk to me about control!" John shot back. "I told you gambling was bad news. Everyone told you. But no, you were so smart. You knew what you were doing."

"Keep your voice down," Keith cautioned frantically.

"You're nothing but an addict," John said with disgust, turning his sweaty back again.

Keith was desperate. Making the football team had made him larger than life, had made him popular and confident, had made campus rulers such as John Badillo accept him as a friend. Now all of that was on the line, and there was no way out. If Keith didn't throw this game, he was going to have to answer to some pretty tough characters. The truth was, he was terrified. John had to help him.

"So, what was it like?" he whispered to John, scooting closer on the bench. "I mean, having Victoria again after all this time?"

"You slime!" John said, spinning around. "It wasn't like that and you know it. I thought Katia was dying! I was out of my mind! What happened between me and Victoria was nothing. It didn't mean a thing."

The sad thing was, Keith believed him. He'd been one of the many who had warned his sister about

John, of course, but this time he really believed Badillo was getting a bad break. Unfortunately, it didn't change what he had to do.

"Just remember this," Keith said, his brown eyes growing hard. "You have a pretty ugly track record. If push comes to shove, Katia will believe what I tell her. Now, do we have a deal or what?"

John didn't answer—there was nothing to say. They both knew Keith had won.

"I'm glad I ran into you, Suzanne," Luke said. "I'm not much in the mood for football. I don't even like it on a good day."

"And it's not a good day, is it?"

Luke just shook his head.

From the moment she had crossed the parking lot and gotten a good look into Luke's gorgeous blue eyes, Suzanne had known instinctively that something was very wrong. She wanted so desperately to know what it was, to help him if she could, but first she had to find a way to get him alone.

"The game is your basic disaster," she told him, thinking fast. "They're creaming us. I was just about to go for a walk to see the fall colors. Want to come?"

"I'd like to," he said. "But Nikki's expecting me. I'm already late."

Was it her imagination, or had he hesitated? She decided to press her advantage.

"Well, I'm sure she'll be glad to see you," Suzanne said slowly, choosing her words carefully. "You can't miss her—she's sitting in a big crowd with Katia and Deb and Victoria."

"Great," he groaned.

"I know," Suzanne commiserated. "It *is* kind of a scene."

For a moment they stood there, Suzanne fidgeting uncomfortably, Luke looking with loathing toward the bleachers.

"Well, maybe just a quick walk," he said at last, smiling for the first time since she'd spotted him. "Since you asked so nicely."

Suzanne couldn't believe her luck—her plan had worked!

But once they wandered away from school and onto the deserted streets, the leaves overhead vivid shades of red and gold, Luke grew quiet. As they walked, Suzanne wanted to take his hand, to ask him what was wrong, but she didn't dare. Every now and then the roar of the crowd at the high school far behind them cut the quiet like a rush of wind or a wave crashing on the beach. Suzanne felt as if they were the only two people left in the world, the world away from Hillcrest High.

Luke broke the silence between them. "I'm so glad I ran into you."

"Do you want to talk about why you're so bummed out?" Suzanne asked, relieved that Luke had spoken at last.

"I don't know. I don't want to load you down with my problems," Luke said. He sounded so sad.

Impulsively Suzanne reached out and took his arm, pulling him closer and slipping her hand into his jacket pocket. As her cold fingers laced through his, she felt the same tingle she had the night they'd kissed. "I want to hear your problems," she said. "I mean, if you want to tell me about them."

Luke laughed bitterly. "How much time do you have?"

"However much it takes," she assured him. "Listen, Luke, I know what it's like to think there's no one you can turn to. Everyone else here is so happy and so well-off. I . . . well . . . there's some kind of link between us, I guess." Suzanne paused, afraid she had said too much. "What I mean is, I'm here for you. If you want me."

She held her breath as Luke considered.

"Yeah," he said at last. "Thanks. I think if anyone could understand, you could."

"That's it," Victoria said as she watched John throw a do-or-die pass over the head of every player in the end zone. "The final nail in the coffin. I've never seen John play so badly in my life."

"They could still pull it off," Katia said hopefully, checking the time left on the scoreboard clock.

"Please," Victoria said, shuddering. "Not even Deb could be that naive."

Deb ignored Victoria's insult. "I'm afraid she's right," she said to Katia. "This game is history."

"Of course I'm right," Victoria said. "I'm always right."

Sometimes hanging around with Deb and Katia really got on Victoria's nerves. Every time Victoria looked at Katia, she was still glad that Katia hadn't been killed in her BMW that night, but she *was* only a sophomore. And ever since Katia had started dating John, it was as though the rest of her brain had been put on hold. And then there was Deb. Deb was always so annoyingly nice, so unrelentingly normal, that sometimes it drove Victoria crazy.

"Earth to Nikki," Victoria said, waving a hand in front of her best friend's face. "Come in, Nikki."

"What?" Nikki asked, startled.

"I was just explaining that this game is totally finished. We might as well go home and get ready for the dance tonight."

"Don't you think we ought to stay until it's over?"

"I hate to break it to you, Nik, but it *is* over," Victoria said, standing up.

Nikki didn't move. "You guys go ahead," she said distantly. "I'm going to wait for Luke a little longer."

Victoria tossed her wavy red hair. "If he isn't here by now, he probably isn't coming. Even if he is, he doesn't deserve to find you waiting."

"I'm going to wait a few more minutes," Nikki insisted. "I'll see you at the dance."

"Fine. Suit yourself," Victoria huffed, gathering her things.

Nikki used to be a blast to hang out with, Victoria thought, but lately she's been down all the time. Victoria had tried to be sympathetic, had tried to help her out, but now it was just getting boring. As she made her way to the stairs, Victoria took one last look back at her friend. The bleachers were emptying and Nikki was sitting alone, her usually

21

sunny face set in a vacant stare, her blue eyes worried. Deb was helping Katia navigate the aisle with her cast and crutches. And was Katia actually *crying?* She *was!* Over a football game. Victoria sighed. I've got to find some new people to hang out with or I'm going to go out of my mind, she thought.

Nikki couldn't pretend any longer that Luke was coming. The stands were practically empty, and it was starting to get dark. She shivered in her new leather jacket.

I'm going to count to ten, she told herself, and then if he doesn't come, I'm out of here. But she didn't count—instead she sat there and wondered what she was doing. Nikki knew she should go home. After all, she trusted Luke. For the two years they'd been together, he'd never given her any reason not to.

Except for one—one brunette who'd left the stadium before halftime had even begun. Nikki struggled to push that thought from her mind. Luke would have a good reason for not coming to the game, she told herself, and they'd have a great time at the dance. So why was she so worried?

"Nikki! Nikki, I can't believe you're still here!" Luke called.

Nikki's heart leaped at the sound of his voice. She rushed down the stairs and threw herself into his arms.

"You're here!" she said, kissing him hungrily. "I knew you'd come!" It felt so good to hold him, to nuzzle her cold face against his warm neck.

"I got held up at work," Luke said. "I can't

believe you waited for me. You must be freezing!"

"But you'll warm me up, won't you?" Nikki asked suggestively, squeezing him tighter. Soon she was lost in his kisses, all of her worries behind her. What an idiot she'd been. "Come on!" she said suddenly, pulling him toward the parking lot. "I want to go home and change before the dance."

"What for? You look great," he said.

"C'mon, let's go to my house," Nikki insisted.

Luke hesitated, then said, "Okay, sure. Let's go."

Nikki started her yellow Jeep with a roar. She couldn't wait to have Luke to herself, and as she drove quickly through the darkening downtown streets, she imagined the great night ahead of them.

She would wear her blue strapless dress, the one that matched her eyes and showed off her long legs. This was going to be a very special occasion. Nikki would make sure of that!

Her thoughts were suddenly interrupted as her headlights illuminated a red mountain bike being pedaled at top speed along the side of the road. It was Suzanne, her long brown hair streaming out behind her. Nikki groaned internally as she glanced at Luke, whose eyes were fixed intently on Suzanne's straining back. At least Nikki hoped that was what he was looking at.

"She's out riding late," Nikki remarked, trying to keep it light.

"Who?" Luke asked, looking quickly forward.

"Suzanne. Didn't you see her?"

"No." He fiddled nervously with the vents in the dashboard.

Nikki felt as if someone had sucked all the air out of the car. Luke was lying—he had to be! But why? She watched as he squirmed uncomfortably in the passenger seat, trying to smile.

There was only one explanation: a guilty conscience. He'd been with Suzanne all afternoon! Why else would she be riding her bike through town this late? In that fraction of a second, Nikki knew that things between her and Luke would never be the same again.

Three

"What the heck happened out there, Badillo?" Coach Kostro raged, slamming his fist down hard on the old metal desk. "A team of nine-year-old girls plays better football than that! I've never seen such a sorry spectacle in my life! You were pitiful. Do you hear me? Pitiful!" His shouts echoed around the glassed-in cubicle that served as his locker-room office.

"Yes, Coach," John said, too ashamed to meet the coach's eyes. The way Coach Kostro was carrying on, John was pretty sure the whole school had heard him. He prayed there weren't too many guys still hanging around their lockers.

"Well, what do you have to say for yourself?"

"I don't know. I guess I had a bad day," John admitted.

"A bad day?" Kostro exploded. "A bad day? That's like calling World War Two a little tiff. You had a *stinking* day, Badillo. Stinking! Do you hear me?"

"Yes, Coach," John said, his eyes still fixed on his muddy white game shoes.

"You ever play that way again and you're going to warm the bench for the rest of the season! Am I making myself clear?"

"But Coach—"

"But nothing! Now get your sorry butt out of my office."

John left the office in a silent fury, but it wasn't Coach Kostro he was angry with. The coach was right—he did stink. He'd be lucky ever to play again after this, and it was all Keith's fault.

"Hey, John, how'd it go?" Keith was already showered and waiting for him next to his locker, trying to look casual.

"Don't give me that," John snapped. "You know how it went—the whole school knows! You'd better keep out of my face for a while."

"Ah, come on, man," Keith said. "It's over now."

"Maybe for you," John shouted. "You got what you wanted, didn't you?"

Keith tried to hush him.

"Just remember," John continued in a rage. "If you ever say one thing against me to Katia, I'm coming after you. Everyone in Hillcrest is going to know what happened here today."

"Could you keep your voice down?" Keith begged.

"No, I can't," John yelled, getting louder by the second. "If you can't take it, you'd better get away from me like I told you to!"

Finally Keith grabbed his gym bag and slid out

26

of the locker room, leaving John alone. John sank slowly onto a bench and buried his mud-streaked face in his tired hands. Every part of his body ached, and scenes from the afternoon's beating still played before his eyes like a horror movie. He couldn't believe what he'd done. All the hard work, all his dreams of being a pro—it was humiliating to have played the way he had that day. Now he was going to have to work twice as hard just to earn back the respect he had lost. I did it for love, he told himself. I did it for Katia.

But somehow he wasn't convinced that it made him any better than Keith.

Suzanne pulled her mountain bike up outside the entry to Willis Workout. Every time Suzanne saw the gym, she was still amazed that they were able to afford it. Of course, if Suzanne's father hadn't been secretly helping them with the money . . . She shook her head. There's no point thinking about that right now, she told herself as she pushed through the door of her mother's luxurious office.

"Oh, hi, Suzanne," Valerie Willis said, rising from behind her enormous desk. She looked great in a purple thong leotard with pink tights and white aerobic shoes—an outfit that very few women her age would even have dared try on. "I was just talking about you."

"Oh, yeah?" Suzanne said dryly, plopping into a cream-colored chair.

"Bob Houghton mentioned that Ian was going

to a dance at the high school tonight. Did you know there's a dance?"

"Of course, Mom. Everybody knows about the dance."

"Aren't you going?" Ms. Willis perched lightly on the front edge of her desk.

"No."

"Why not?"

"Well, for one thing, I don't have a date." Suzanne twisted sideways in the chair and dangled her legs over the padded arm.

"Ian doesn't have a date. He's going with his cousin Sally."

"Well, I don't have a cousin, either," Suzanne snapped. "Could we please change the subject?"

"I just think you should go," her mother insisted. "It might be fun. Won't Nikki and all your friends be there?"

All her friends—ha! That was a good one. The last thing Suzanne wanted to do was stand around by herself at a dance and make a big, irresistible target for Nikki and Victoria. But if she didn't go, her mother would suspect that something was wrong, and Suzanne just didn't feel like getting into it with her mother. Anyway, she reminded herself, Luke's going to be there.

Thinking about the afternoon they had just spent together made Suzanne feel tingly all over. The secret things he'd told her—about his mom, about stealing from work—had made the bond between them even stronger than before.

"I can't believe I'm telling you this," Luke had

said, their hands entwined in his warm jacket pocket as they wandered the empty sidewalks. "I've never even told this to Nikki."

"Maybe that's because Nikki doesn't understand you," Suzanne had said, holding her breath to see what he'd say.

He'd laughed. "And you do." It was more of a statement than a question.

"You know I do," she'd told him, moving closer, feeling the electricity between them.

She'd never felt so incredibly drawn to anyone, and she knew he'd felt it, too. If only he had kissed her . . .

"Well? How about it?" her mother asked, jolting Suzanne back to the present.

"Huh?" Suzanne jumped. "How about what?"

"The dance! I think you should go."

"Oh. Right." Suzanne imagined herself wrapped in Luke's strong arms, dancing to some slow, romantic song. Sure, Nikki was going to be there, but Suzanne had a feeling that Nikki's days as Luke's girlfriend were numbered. All it was going to take was a little patience.

"I might as well go," Suzanne said, smiling to herself.

Nikki was furious—it was worse than the night she'd caught Luke with Suzanne at the country club. She paced up and down her living room in a rage while Luke stood helplessly by the sofa.

"I can't believe you went out with her again and then you lied to me about it," she said, choking back tears.

"It wasn't like that, Nikki," Luke pleaded. "We just went for a walk."

"And then you lied about it," she insisted.

"Only because I knew how you'd react. I didn't want to hurt you."

"You didn't want to hurt me by telling the truth, but you don't mind going behind my back," Nikki accused. "That's very big of you."

"Nikki, I'm sorry I lied to you. But you don't understand."

"I understand that you're cheating on me again!"

"No, I'm not. I swear. Nothing like that happened. We just talked. Suzanne's a really nice person."

"Are you stupid? She's been trying to break us up ever since she moved here!" Nikki cried, the tears starting in earnest.

Luke tried to take Nikki into his arms, but she pushed him away. He felt horrible seeing her cry, but horrible in a numb, hollow kind of way. He just couldn't do this anymore. He couldn't keep all of these things inside him. If he and Nikki were going to stay together, she was going to have to deal with his life the way it really was.

"There are lots of things going on that you don't know about, Nikki," he began.

Nikki took a few deep breaths and pushed her blond hair out of her wet face with one trembling hand. "I'm listening," she said.

"I just wasn't in the mood to go to the game—it's been a rough few weeks." Luke paused to choose his words and then plunged ahead. "You know my

30

mom lost her job, and that she drinks. What you don't know is that she's been fired from every job she's ever had, and now she's completely quit looking. It's been weeks since she's brought home enough money to pay the rent, let alone to buy food or anything else. We're way behind, and I won't be surprised if our landlord kicks us out any day now."

"Oh, Luke," Nikki said with true sympathy.

"There's more," Luke said grimly. "My mother calls you a little princess because you live in Hillcrest Hollow, and sometimes I wonder if she's right. Every time I've got a problem, your solution is always for me to skip work and do something fun. I don't work at the record store because I like it, Nikki—I do it because we need the money. Of course I'd rather be shopping or watching videos with you, but most days I don't even have enough money for lunch. And now I'm in trouble at work . . ." His words trailed off. He felt conflicted and exhausted. "Well, you get the picture."

"Luke, why didn't you ever tell me any of this?" Nikki asked, looking truly crushed. "I love you. Didn't you think I'd want to help?"

"I don't know," Luke said, taking her into his arms and smoothing her tangled hair. "I guess I just didn't think you'd understand."

"I wouldn't understand?" Nikki said angrily, pushing back out of his grasp. "But Suzanne would? You don't trust me enough to make me a part of your life, but you don't mind spilling your guts to Suzanne?" She was crying again.

"Nikki . . ." Luke reached for her again.

"No, Luke," she sobbed. "I think you'd better go. I want to be with you, but not if you don't want to be with me—to really be with me. You're a free man. Are you going to fly right into Suzanne's arms now?"

"What are you saying? Are you saying it's over?"

"I'm saying I think we ought to take a break."

Nikki sank onto the huge leather sofa and hugged an embroidered pillow to her chest. Luke could barely stand to see her in so much pain.

"Nikki, I'm sorry I hurt you," he said, sitting beside her. "You know how much I love you."

She started sobbing harder.

"It's just that I don't know what I'm doing anymore," he explained. "How can I be any good to you when I'm no good to myself? Maybe you're right. I think we should each spend some time on our own—at least until I figure things out."

"Fine," Nikki sobbed, clutching her pillow. "I thought we had something special. I'd have done anything for you, Luke." She threw down the pillow and ran from the room.

"I know," Luke whispered to the empty space. He lifted the tear-splotched pillow from the floor and held it to his face for a moment, smelling her perfume. Then he put it gently on the couch and let himself out.

Deb was one of the very first people at the dance, but she was used to that. It seemed as if she was always on the committee for these things. Always on the committee and never with a date.

She sighed. Still, she wasn't going to give up hope. Just because she was the last of her friends to have a boyfriend didn't mean there wasn't someone special out there for her. She took one last look around the gym to make sure that everything was ready.

The first football game and dance of the season were always held on a Saturday. It was supposed to be a big deal, so the dance committee had really knocked itself out, coming up with a great theme. They had ultimately gone with Nikki's idea of "Then and Now." Since most of the kids at Hillcrest High had lived in town since kindergarten, it was easy to come up with photographs—they had pictures of all the football players as kids, pictures of most students as they'd looked in junior high, pictures of the teachers in bell-bottoms and love beads—it was hilarious. Too bad no one would be in the mood to appreciate it.

"Deb! I'm so glad you're here," Katia said, hobbling toward her on her crutches. She was wearing a navy blue dress with a thigh-high white stocking on her left leg and the knee-high white cast on her right. A fuzzy pale pink sock covered her foot below the cast.

"Boy, the gym looks great," Katia added. "Was this your idea?"

"Nikki's," Deb admitted. "We decorated yesterday after school, but I thought she'd have been here by now."

"John's not here yet, either," Katia said, looking worried. "He and Keith were going to come straight from the game, but I haven't seen either one of them. I hope they're not in too much trouble with the coach."

"Why would they be in trouble? It's just a game."

Katia looked at her as if she were crazy. "Just a *game?*" she said. "It was the season opener! Poor John."

Deb had to smile as she noticed whom Katia was reserving most of her sympathy for. It looked as if Keith was on his own.

"I can't understand it," Katia went on. "We should have beaten them by a mile! Oh, there he is!" she exclaimed. John had just walked in the door on the opposite side of the gym, looking surly and depressed. "See you later."

"Later." Deb watched as Katia worked her way to John through the growing crowd, then she went over to tell the DJ to start things up. Soon people were dancing at one end of the darkened gym, while the people who just wanted to hang out and talk had gathered at the other. The noise was incredible.

"Hey, Deb," someone said behind her. Deb turned to see Suzanne, dressed in a clinging red dress that flattered her olive skin and brown hair. Sometimes Deb thought that if Nikki and Suzanne were both blond or both brunette, they'd look a lot alike. They had the same perfectly arched eyebrows and heart-shaped mouth, the same knockout body.

"Hey, Suzanne," Deb said.

"Wow. You're talking to me. What a pleasant surprise!" Suzanne responded, pretending to be shocked.

"It'll probably get me in trouble," Deb admitted. "But *I'm* not mad at you."

"Thanks," Suzanne said gratefully. "Where is Nikki tonight?"

"I was wondering that myself," Deb said. "She should have been here by now."

"And Victoria?"

"Before nine o'clock?" Deb laughed. "You know Victoria. . . . So what do you think of our theme? Isn't it great?"

"Honestly? It's a little hard for me to relate to."

"What do you mean? Nikki thought it would be a blast for everyone to see their old pictures."

Suzanne grimaced. "Well, that's just it, Deb. I'm not in any of those pictures. Kind of on the outside looking in, if you know what I mean. It figures it was Nikki's idea."

Deb didn't understand. Suzanne couldn't really think this was about her, could she? "I don't get it," Deb said.

"If you haven't noticed, Nikki hates me," Suzanne said. "It would be just like her to do this to remind me that I don't belong here."

"I don't think so, Suzanne," Deb said uncomfortably. "Nikki isn't that way."

"No? She thinks I'm trying to steal Luke," Suzanne said.

Now that it was out in the open, it would be a relief to clear it up, Deb thought. "And are you?" she asked.

Suzanne looked away, then back. "Well, the way she's acting, she'd deserve it," she said at last. "Actually,

I was hoping I'd see him here. That's why I came."

Deb didn't know what to say. She wanted to be Suzanne's friend, but she was loyal to Nikki. Better to change the subject.

"*They're* sure not enjoying the party," Deb said, indicating the football players, who were standing in a sullen group along the opposite wall.

A raucous laugh made Deb look in the direction of the refreshments table. It was Sally Ross, cracking everyone up, as usual. But Deb barely saw Sally—she only had eyes for Ian. He was wearing his usual I-don't-care jeans and T-shirt, and his long blond hair was pulled away from his face and tied with a leather thong. Deb was positive he was the most handsome guy in school.

"Not bad, huh?" Suzanne said at her elbow.

"What do you mean?" Deb asked innocently.

Suzanne laughed. "Maybe that innocent act works on Victoria, but I know you better. You have a crush on Ian."

"I do," Deb admitted.

"Why don't you go over and talk to him?" Suzanne suggested.

Deb tried to imagine herself walking up to Ian and starting a conversation, but the picture wouldn't come. Especially not with his cousin Sally standing there. Deb liked Sally, but her sense of humor could be merciless sometimes.

"I don't think so," Deb declined.

"Go on, you look great!" Suzanne encouraged her.

Deb's hand flew to her shoulder-length black hair, which she had styled that night into a smooth

French twist. She knew she was pretty, but there were so many pretty girls in Hillcrest. And after all, if Victoria had failed with Ian . . .

"You're not Victoria," Suzanne said, reading her mind. "And believe it or not, she's not God's gift to the men of this planet. Don't tell her, though—it will only crush her overgrown ego."

Deb giggled. "Nikki said Ian might be able to use his computer to help me find my birth parents. You know, look for hospital records and things like that."

"What a great idea!" Suzanne said.

"Do you really think so?"

"Yeah," Suzanne said. "Much as I hate to admit it, given the source. You know, if Ian's half as nice as my mom thinks his dad is, he'll be happy to help you out. And even if he can't, at least it will give you something to talk about. Now go!"

"I don't know. . . ." Deb's heart was pounding with excitement despite her protest. "What should I say?"

"How about, 'Hi, I'm Deb. How do you like me so far?'"

Deb laughed nervously. "Yeah, right. No, really, Suzanne," she pleaded. "What am I going to say to him?"

Suzanne tossed her head impatiently. "I don't know, Deb. Just be yourself—you'll think of something."

Deb looked over to where Ian was standing with Sally, and even though the music was getting louder with every song, all she could hear was the blood rushing in her ears. *I must be crazy,* she told herself as she took her first slow, tentative step in Ian's direction.

Four

Ian Houghton was bored out of his mind. I can't be-lieve I let Sally talk me into this, he thought, looking around the gym. It was all so . . . pointless. A few peo-ple were dancing, but nearly everyone else was stand-ing around in little cliques talking and trying to look cool. The big topic of conversation for the evening seemed to be football and how much the home team stank. It was mind-numbing. He was just about to tell Sally that they had to leave when he caught sight of a beautiful African-American girl walking his way.

He knew who she was—Deb Johnson. He'd seen her often with that pain in the butt Victoria Hill and her friends, but he'd never talked to her. Maybe he was imagining it, but she'd always seemed so differ-ent from the others. So much more caring, so much more real. You ought to talk to her, he told himself.

He watched as Deb approached the refresh-ments table and asked for a diet soda. She was so pretty, and he loved the way she dressed. Nice, but sensible—not like her conceited friends. That night, for example, she was wearing a plain white suit that looked great with her dark skin. Deb got her soda and stood for a moment by the table, only twenty feet from where he was standing.

Go on, man, he thought, now's your big chance. But Ian didn't move. He hated meeting people in person; it was so much easier on the Internet.

Deb started to walk away.

You blew it, he told himself, disgusted. But wait a minute—was she looking his way? Yes, and she was coming toward him!

"Hi. I'm Deb," she said shyly, barely looking up. "You're Ian, right?"

"Right," he said, too amazed to think of anything more intelligent. "Uh, how's it going?"

Deb nodded. "Fine. Great party, isn't it?"

"Yeah!" he agreed enthusiastically. "Really great."

There was an awkward silence between them.

"So, Deb," Ian tried at last, desperate for something to say. "I've noticed you around school."

"You have?" Deb asked, looking up and smiling. She was gorgeous when she smiled. Then suddenly she seemed to become confused and dropped her gaze again.

"Oh, of course," she said, addressing her diet soda. "You mean because I'm a friend of Victoria's."

"I promise not to hold that against you," Ian joked. Now that he had officially met her, he was more determined than ever to get to know her. "Are you into computers?" he asked.

"Sure," Deb said. "That is, I really only know the basics, but I'm learning. Everyone says you're really good with them."

"I hack," Ian said modestly.

Deb took a deep breath. "Do you think if someone was adopted, you could find out who their birth parents were?"

"With the computer? I don't know. Maybe."

Ian sensed the conversation had suddenly become serious, but he wasn't sure why. Deb looked even more shy and uncomfortable than before, as if she wished she could run away.

"I could try," he added, hoping to keep her from leaving. "I'd be glad to try, in fact. Do you know someone who's adopted?"

"Me," Deb said quietly, and then she seemed to lose her nerve completely. "Oh, this is so embarrassing. I don't even know you, and here I am telling you my whole life story. Like you don't have better things to do with your time than look for my birth parents! I'm sorry—I'd better go." She turned to leave.

Ian's hand shot out involuntarily. The next thing he knew, it had closed gently but insistently around Deb's small wrist, stopping her progress and drawing her closer.

"Don't go," he said.

"Hey, Stein! Fumble any footballs lately?" yelled someone in the crowd.

Keith squinted in the darkened gym, trying to spot the guy with the smart mouth, but he couldn't. The coward was hiding.

40

"Why don't you come over here and ask me to my face?" Keith countered hotly. This had been going on all night.

"Ooh," breathed the crowd, as if they were scared, but he knew it was all just a big joke to them.

The truth was, he felt lousy. If the team had won, he'd have been a hero. All the guys would be slapping him on the back and all the girls would want to dance with him. As it was, he was an outcast. He was hanging out against the wall with the rest of the football team, but he might as well have been standing in Siberia. John was smooching with Katia in a corner—coming up for air only long enough to shoot Keith the occasional dirty look—and none of the other players was too high on John at the moment, either.

Keith felt guilty, but he still didn't know what choice he'd had. *I did what I had to do*, he assured himself for the hundredth time. *There was no other way.*

He'd hoped to see Nikki, but it seemed as if she and Luke weren't coming. If anyone could have cheered him up, it would have been her. Nikki . . . lately she was even more on his mind than usual. He tried not to think about her, but it was impossible. Luke didn't know how good he had it.

Keith's thoughts were interrupted as Victoria made her grand entrance. She'd come in through the door on the other side, near the DJ, and now she stood inside the entrance fussing with her hair, making sure every strand was perfect. Keith watched as she smoothed her short red skirt against the front of her toned thighs, bending over just enough to make sure he got a good look at the cleavage beneath her sheer black blouse. Victoria never changed—she was still as self-absorbed as ever. She'd practically driven Keith crazy those few weeks they'd dated the year before. On the other hand, she was outrageously good-looking.

Suddenly Keith felt an overwhelming urge to ask her to dance, kind of for old times' sake. When he'd been dating Victoria, he'd been at his peak, on top of the world. And I will be again, he told himself. This is all behind me now. There would be other football games to win—other card games, too. Everyone would get over it when he played great the next week. He crossed to where Victoria was standing by the dance floor.

"What's a hot girl like you doing in a dumb place like this?" he asked.

Victoria smiled flirtatiously. "A question I often ask myself," she said.

Keith's pulse quickened. She was talking to him! Things were definitely starting to look up.

The DJ put on a slow song.

"Do you want to dance?" Keith asked immediately.

"Why not?" Victoria said, leading the way.

By the time they'd danced to a couple of songs, Keith was feeling pretty good. Victoria was totally leading him on, and he didn't care why she was doing it. If she was lonely that night, then he was just as lonely—stranger things had happened. Which reminded him . . .

"Hey, you won't believe who Ian Houghton's hitting on," he told her, shouting over the music. Still dancing, he pointed toward the other end of the gym. "Check out your buddy Deb."

"What?" Victoria screeched, stopping right in the middle of the song. But at exactly that moment, Ian and Deb slipped out the main door and into the parking lot.

"Aw, you just missed it," Keith said. "I said, Ian Houghton and Deb Johnson—"

"I heard you the first time!" Victoria snapped, storming off the dance floor.

"Victoria! Hey, wait up." Keith ran after her as she pushed through the crowd, heading for the door that Deb had just gone out. "What did I say?"

They were both almost to the exit when two police officers came in from outside.

"Stay right where you are," one of the officers said. "Are you Keith Stein?"

"Yes," Keith admitted, feeling suddenly ill. "What's up?"

"I got a warrant here for your arrest. Will you turn around and put your hands on the wall, please?"

Keith heard Victoria gasp behind him as he turned.

"But what did he do, Officer?" she asked.

"Your boyfriend here is charged with aiding and abetting an illegal gambling scheme. You didn't really think anyone could play that bad by accident, did you?"

Keith panicked as he felt the cold metal cuffs close over his wrists.

"You're arresting me because I had a bad game?"

he asked. "This is some kind of a joke, right?" He tried to laugh, but it came out more like a wheeze.

"If I were you," the officer advised him, "I'd exercise my right to remain silent. We know all about your bookie friend Tony. In fact, he's sitting in a comfy holding cell right now."

Keith felt sick. A huge crowd had gathered, and someone had turned the lights back up.

"I got the other one," the second officer said, returning to the group and pushing a handcuffed John in front of him.

Keith could hear his sister sobbing somewhere at the back of the crowd, unable to get through on her crutches.

"John!" Katia screamed. "John, what's happening?"

The officers began reading them their rights, but to Keith it all seemed like a bad dream. He saw the crowd part as Katia finally made her way to the front, saw her pretty face twist in horror as she realized it was her brother as well as her boyfriend, and after that Keith's mind went numb.

Victoria stood shivering in the parking lot as the police car pulled away. The cold wind cut right through her thin blouse and short skirt, but someone had to stay with Katia.

"I don't believe it," Katia sobbed into her shoulder, completely undone.

Victoria smoothed Katia's long auburn hair. "Come on, Katia," she soothed. "This is all some bizarre mistake. The guys will be fine."

"How can you be sure?" Katia whimpered.

"I just am," Victoria said. "They're big boys."
But her mind was barely on the subject. Instead
she was fighting an overwhelming feeling of *déjà
vu*. Standing with an injured Katia outside in the
cold, the revolving lights of the police cars illumi-
nating the dark parking lot with eerie blue and yellow flashes, Victoria was reminded of another
night—a night when the police *hadn't* caught their
man. The night of that horrible car accident. She
shuddered involuntarily and pulled Katia closer.

"Nobody's going to hurt you," she said protectively.

"What?" Katia sniffled, lifting her tearstained
face.

Victoria started as she realized her mistake. "I
mean, they'll be fine," she covered. "C'mon, I'll take
you home."

"My parents are going to kill Keith!" Katia
cried, beginning to sob again. "How could he have
done this? And John . . . why?"

"You're getting hysterical," Victoria said softly.
"You've got to calm down or you aren't going to help
anyone. Can you do that?" She continued stroking
Katia's hair until Katia nodded into her shoulder.
"Okay, then. Take some deep breaths. Better?"

Katia nodded, wiping at her eyes with the back
of her hand.

"Then let's go."

Victoria helped Katia back onto her crutches
and guided her to the white Porsche convertible her
father had bought her after he'd totaled her vintage
BMW—an unspoken attempt to buy her silence

45

that disgusted Victoria every time she saw it. She opened the passenger door and carefully helped Katia in, wedging the crutches behind the seats as best she could. Seeing Katia sitting there, so little and helpless, the sense of *déjà vu* came rushing back as once again Victoria pictured that other night—and Katia in another car.

"Buckle your seat belt," Victoria ordered.

By the time they pulled up to the Steins' big Victorian house, Katia seemed a lot calmer. She grabbed Victoria's hand tightly before she could get out of the car.

"Thanks," Katia said gratefully, her brown eyes swollen from crying. "I don't know what I'd do without you."

"It was nothing," Victoria said, suddenly uncomfortable. She glanced involuntarily at the cast on Katia's leg. Katia probably would be doing a lot better without her. At least she'd never found out about Victoria and John kissing in her hospital room that time. It had hurt like crazy to give John up again, but it would have been horrible to lose them both.

"No, I mean it, Victoria," Katia insisted. "You're a true friend."

"Is that you, Deb?" Mrs. Johnson called from the living room. "How was the dance?"

"Heaven!" Deb said, walking in to join her family. She and Ian had left early and gone out for ice cream. Aside from being drop-dead gorgeous, he was so nice! She couldn't believe how willing he'd been to help her with her problem.

46

"Hey, Poppy!" she said as her cocker spaniel charged over to meet her. "Did you keep Ted in line like I told you?"

"Very funny," her little brother said, looking up from the carpet in front of the television.

"Just kidding, bro," Deb said.

"You're in a good mood tonight," Mr. Johnson remarked, lowering his newspaper.

"I met this incredible guy," Deb enthused. "He's cute and he's smart. . . ."

"Deborah's got a crush," Ted sang.

"Do not," Deb said, but she giggled when she said it. Do too, she thought.

"So who is this boy?" Mrs. Johnson asked.

"His name is Ian Houghton," Deb answered, savoring the chance to say his name out loud. "He's going to show me how to use the Internet."

"The Internet!" her dad protested. "When I tried to show you, you said it was boring. What's this sudden interest in the Net?"

Too late, Deb realized her mistake. She was so happy, she'd just been babbling on without caution. She couldn't tell her parents what she wanted with the Internet; it would devastate them. She knew they loved her as much as anyone's birth parents ever had—more, judging from her friends' dysfunctional families—and there was no way she was ever going to leave them. But where she came from, who her blood family was, was a big part of her. She had to know.

"Well, it just seems like fun now," she managed at last.

"Stan!" her mother said. "Don't give her such a hard time. Can't you see the Internet is just an excuse? I'm sure that when Ian shows her the Net, it will be very interesting."

Deb breathed a secret sigh of relief but pretended to be embarrassed, as if her mom had found her out.

"I'm going up to bed now," she said, kissing her parents good night.

Deb was in a happy daze as she put on an oversized pink T-shirt and climbed under the covers. All she could think about was Ian and the fact that she was finally going to do something to find out where she had come from.

And Ian. She'd never seen eyes like his in her life. She had always thought that Luke's blue eyes were intense, but when Ian fixed her with his green ones, it was as if he could read her mind.

It seemed to Deb that she'd been waiting to have a boyfriend all her life. She'd always stood forgotten on the sidelines while Nikki went steady with Luke and Victoria dated guy after guy. Even Katia Stein had a boyfriend now, and she was only a sophomore. But somehow Deb's Mr. Right had never come along. At least, not until that night.

Deb smiled happily in the darkness. This could be the guy, her heart kept insisting. Ian could be the one.

Five

On Sunday morning Suzanne rose late and took her time getting dressed. The dance the night before had been a total waste of time as far as seeing Luke was concerned, but it definitely hadn't lacked excitement overall. Everyone there had been totally shocked by the arrest of Keith and John.

Suzanne wondered if the guys were home yet and how much trouble they were in. She felt as if she ought to do something to help, but she didn't know what. For all she knew, *they* weren't speaking to her, either. Everything was so complicated now.

This is all Nikki's fault! she thought angrily, stomping down the stairs. If Nikki weren't so immature, Suzanne wouldn't be on the outs with everyone. More than that, she missed her father . . . *their* father. It wasn't fair of Nikki to come between them now that Suzanne had finally gotten to know him a little.

She brooded as she ate her cereal. Her mother

49

was already at work, of course, so there was no one to talk to. For a while Suzanne toyed with the idea of riding her bike over to the Tunesmith to talk to Luke, but then she decided against it. The last thing he needed was to get into any more trouble at work.

Of course, she could pretend to buy something. No, it was stupid. Instead she decided just to take a ride and see where her pedals led her.

Soon she was whizzing through the brisk fall air on her way to the ritzy Hillcrest Hollow part of town. Just for the scenery, she told herself. It wasn't until she pulled into Nikki's driveway that Suzanne admitted to herself that she'd been headed there all along. With her heart in her throat, she pressed the doorbell and heard it chime inside.

"Suzanne!" Mr. Stewart said, answering the door himself. "What a pleasant surprise!" He was still in his bathrobe and some ratty corduroy slippers, but it didn't seem to bother him.

"Hi," Suzanne said, instantly glad she had come. By his reaction it was obvious that her father was still in the dark about her fight with Nikki. "Are you here all by yourself?" she asked.

"Helen's not home, but Nikki's in her room," Mr. Stewart said. "Let me call her."

"No!" Suzanne said quickly. "I mean, call her in a minute. I . . . was hoping to spend some time with you alone."

"You were?" he said, a surprised but friendly smile lighting up his features. "Well, that's great. Do you drink coffee?" he asked, leading her into the kitchen. "I was just having some myself."

"No, but I'd love a glass of water." It had been a fast ride over.

"Coming up," he said, filling the glass and placing it on the kitchen table across from his newspaper and half-empty mug. He sat down and looked at her expectantly.

But now that Suzanne had him alone, she couldn't think of anything to say. "So, how are things at the studio?" she asked to get the ball rolling.

He shrugged. "Not bad. You know how it is."

"Not really," Suzanne admitted, "but I'd like to. I want to be an actress someday, you know. Right now I'm playing the lead in *West Side Story* at school."

Mr. Stewart smiled. "I remember you and Nikki rehearsing for the audition. But I hope you have a fallback plan. Acting is a tough business—not everybody makes it."

"I know," Suzanne said grimly. In fact, nobody knew that better than she.

Her father's face fell. "Oh, no!" he said, realizing his mistake. "I wasn't talking about your mother—"

"It's all right," Suzanne said, cutting him off. "She's happy now."

"Is she?" he asked, and Suzanne could tell he really cared. "I'd like to think she's happy. Things could have been so great between us. . . ." He seemed lost in thought for a moment. "And if you ever need anything, anything at all, I hope you know you can always come to me."

"Thanks. That means a lot."

Her father paused, as if choosing his words carefully. "I'd give anything if—" he began.

51

"Daddy, what are you doing in here?" Nikki interrupted, walking in through the patio door in a brand-new running outfit.

Mr. Stewart jumped. "Nikki! Hi! Look who's here," he said guiltily, gesturing toward Suzanne. "I was just going to call you."

"Hi, Nikki." Suzanne stood up, her heart racing. If only Nikki would talk to her, Suzanne knew, they could work things out.

But Nikki kept her distance, glaring openly at Suzanne while Mr. Stewart fidgeted lamely with his coffee mug. Suzanne could tell he was so worried that Nikki had overheard their conversation that he was oblivious to everything else.

"How nice," Nikki said finally, ice in her voice.

"Yes, well," Mr. Stewart said, "I'll just leave you two to your girl talk, then. I've got plenty of things to do in the study." He picked up his mug and made his escape.

"What are you doing here?" Nikki demanded the instant he'd left. "How dare you show your face in this house?"

"Nikki, come on," Suzanne began. "Don't you think you're going a little far?"

"A little far?" Nikki repeated angrily, the color rising in her cheeks. "What would you know about going a *little* far?"

"What are you talking about?" Suzanne asked. "Can't we just make up and be friends again? I don't want to fight with you."

"You should have thought of that when you were with Luke yesterday!" Nikki yelled. With a

52

visible effort she lowered her voice. "I hope you got what you wanted."

"We just went for a walk!" Suzanne protested.

"You broke us up and you know it!" Nikki accused.

Suzanne was stunned. "You and Luke broke up?"

"Don't play dumb with me," Nikki raged. "This is all your fault. Well, you listen to me, Suzanne Willis. If you think you can hang on to Luke, then take your best shot. But you'd better keep away from me and my family or I'll tell my father all about you."

"What are you talking about?"

"Don't think I haven't noticed the way you're getting all chummy with my dad. It's not normal. If you don't stay away from us, I'm going to tell him that you don't know who your father is because your own mother doesn't even know. I'm going to tell him that your mother used to sleep with every derelict in New York—professionally! Your father is probably the biggest sleaze on the face of the earth."

"You know what, Nikki?" Suzanne countered, furious. "I think you *should* tell your dad about me. Go ahead and tell him that exact story—I dare you! Why don't you do it right now?"

"I'll do it when I'm good and ready," Nikki retorted. "Now get out of my house and don't come back."

"With pleasure!" Suzanne stormed out.

Keith sighed with relief as he finally reached the courthouse lobby and his parents came into view. Sure, they were going to be furious, but at least he was out of jail. John had barely said two words to him all night, and Tony's only greeting had been a threat about what was going to happen to him if he ever opened his mouth. The rest of the guys in the holding cell had been a bunch of drunken losers. All in all, it had been the worst twenty-four hours of Keith's life.

He dropped his eyes in shame as he went to meet his family. By now the police would have told them the whole story of how they'd been following Tony's gambling racket—how the tip they'd received about the rigged football game was just the piece of evidence they'd needed. By now his parents would know that he'd been gambling in a big way. His social life was probably over forever.

He ran a nervous hand through his rumpled brown curls and tried a weak smile on Katia, but the look on her face stopped him cold. The previous night's tears had been replaced by indignant fury. Obviously she knew everything, too.

"I hope you're proud of yourself," Mr. Stein said loudly, in a voice that meant just the opposite. "As if we haven't suffered enough lately."

On the other side of the lobby, Keith could see John talking with his attorney father. At least John will have a good lawyer, he thought, but he knew that Mr. Badillo was probably mortified at the thought of defending his own son. Especially in a town as small as Hillcrest—everyone was going to know.

"If you'll come this way, Mr. Stein," the corrections officer said to Keith's father, "we have a couple of things for you to sign."

"I'll be back," Mr. Stein said in a threatening voice, leaving Keith alone with his mother and Katia.

"Oh, Keith, how could you?" his mother cried as soon as they were alone. "Do you know how much you've hurt your father?"

That figured. As usual, this was going to be all about them. Ever since Katia's accident, Keith had been *persona non grata* around the Stein residence—his parents blamed him for everything.

"I'm sorry," he said automatically.

"So it's true, then," Katia challenged. "You and John rigged the game."

"Katia . . . ," Keith began, but she was already on her way across the room toward John, who was also waiting for his father to sign him out.

"How much did you make on it?" Katia accused John in a voice that echoed down the halls. "Is money so important to you that you would stoop to something like this? Everybody warned me, but I thought I knew you better."

"Kat, let me explain."

"Don't 'Kat' me," she raged. "I should have listened to my brother."

"To your brother?" John retorted, becoming angry himself. "Oh, yeah, Keith is a saint. Let me tell you something about your precious brother—this whole thing is his fault! He made me do it to save his own pathetic butt."

"He *made* you," Katia sneered. "I always thought you had a mind of your own."

"I do, but—" John stopped in midsentence.

"But what?" Katia challenged.

55

John didn't answer.

"But what? What could my brother possibly have over you to make you do something so stupid?"

Keith watched as the truth finally hit Katia. He desperately wished he were anywhere else.

"It's another girl, isn't it?" she gasped. "Oh, no. Everyone told me to watch out for you, but I wouldn't listen." She was crying now.

"It wasn't like that," John pleaded, reaching out to her. "You were so sick and—"

"While I was in the hospital?" Katia exploded in disbelief. "I'm practically dying, and you're out fooling around?"

"No! No, Katia," John said. "That's why it happened—*because* I thought you were dying. I was so upset—we were all going crazy. We were only consoling each other. I swear it didn't mean anything."

"Consoling each other?" Katia repeated. "Are you telling me I know her?"

Keith couldn't turn away as the next awful piece of the puzzle fell into place.

"Oh, no, it was you and Victoria, wasn't it?" she cried. "That's great. Maybe she wishes she had slammed into the tree a little harder."

"Katia, please," John begged. "I . . . I love you. I've never said that to a girl before."

But Katia wasn't listening as she hobbled from the lobby in tears of humiliation. When Keith's parents finally led him out the door to temporary freedom, the last thing he saw was John's murderous stare.

*   *   *

"Am I early?" Deb asked shyly as Ian opened the door.

"Not at all," he said. "Late, if anything."

"Late!" Deb said, alarmed. She pushed up the cuff of her oxford-cloth shirt and checked her watch. "I don't understand it. This watch has always kept good time. . . ."

"I'm kidding," Ian said. "I'm glad you're here."

"Oh," Deb said, relieved. "Me too." In fact, she had barely slept the night before, thinking about seeing Ian.

She followed him into a modern, European-style kitchen, where he grabbed a couple of oranges and three bottles of imported water out of the refrigerator. "I'm always thirsty," he explained.

Deb smiled acknowledgment. "I love your house," she said, looking around the room.

"Thanks. It's my dad's design. So, are you ready to get started?"

"Sure thing," Deb said. "Whenever you are."

Ian led the way up the stairs to his room. Walking behind him, Deb tried to keep her mind on the task ahead of them and her eyes off the seat of Ian's jeans, but it was pretty tough going. For the millionth time she wondered what it would be like to be Ian's girlfriend.

"You know, I've never hacked my way onto a hospital computer before," he admitted. "Here. I brought a chair up from the kitchen for you. It's pretty comfortable."

Deb sat down and faced the computer. "Thanks," she said shyly.

"No problem," he said, dropping into his own black leather desk chair and nudging the mouse to reactivate the monitor display. "I've been trying all morning to figure out the best way to go about this," he told her. "I've got to tell you, though, it seems kind of impossible right now."

Deb's disappointment must have shown on her face.

"But don't get discouraged," Ian reassured her. "I'm not giving up—it just might take a few days, is all."

Suddenly Deb felt guilty at the thought of taking up so much of his time. He must have homework and all sorts of other things to do. It wasn't right of her to ask him to do this.

"Ian," she began, "you don't have to—"

"No sweat," he interrupted, looking at her with those incredible eyes. "I love a good challenge."

Six

Nikki walked into drama rehearsal before school on Monday morning with a world-class chip on her shoulder. It was almost too much to take. The only reason Suzanne had won the lead part of Maria in the first place was that she'd been so obvious about singing that love song to Luke. There's no way I could have sung well after watching that, Nikki rationalized, trying to block the mental picture of her own disastrous audition.

Melissa Pressman had landed the only other good female role—Anita—and Nikki was stuck with the bit part of Rosalia. It's not fair! she thought. She had seriously considered dropping out of the play altogether, but she wouldn't give Suzanne the satisfaction.

Nikki was willing to admit that Suzanne had a good voice—okay, a very good voice. But Nikki's was just as good. It burned her up.

"I don't know how much more of this I can take," Nikki whispered to Jeannie Jensen. Jeannie played Consuelo, another bit part, and the two girls were waiting in the wings of the auditorium while Suzanne held center stage. As usual.

"What do you mean?" Jeannie whispered back.

Nikki gestured toward the singing Suzanne, who was putting everything she had into the big love scene duet, "One Hand, One Heart," with Jason King, the guy who was playing Tony.

"Every time she practices this piece, it's like she thinks she's Natalie Wood," Nikki said, naming the actress who played Maria in the original *West Side Story* movie.

Jeannie giggled, then quickly slapped a hand over her mouth. "She's not that bad. You're exaggerating." She turned toward center stage, where Suzanne and Jason were rehearsing.

"And anyway," Jeannie added, sighing, "Jason King is a dream. I wish I were playing Maria."

Suddenly Nikki had an evil idea. Jeannie Jensen was one of the biggest gossips in school. Anything juicy Jeannie heard was always public record by the end of the day. Before she thought another second, Nikki plunged ahead.

"She wouldn't act like such a hotshot if everybody knew who she really was," Nikki whispered to Jeannie, assuming an air of monumental secrecy.

Jeannie was immediately hooked. "What do you mean?"

Nikki stalled, pretending to have second thoughts.

"I don't know if I should say anything," she said at last.

Jeannie was practically panting. "Are you kidding?" she whispered urgently. "You can trust me."

"Well, okay, then," said Nikki. "It's just that Suzanne's father . . ."

Suzanne knew that something was going on in the wings, but from her spot onstage she couldn't tell what. It wasn't unusual for people to whisper when their character wasn't in the scene being rehearsed—there wasn't much else for them to do—but this was different. She could feel the eyes boring into her, watching her every move.

At first she tried to ignore it, but it became more and more obvious. It seemed as if the entire cast was whispering and staring at her. What could they possibly be talking about? She looked toward Mr. Cadenza, who pounded incompetently away on the piano, oblivious to any disturbance. He clearly enjoyed playing, but it was a good thing the school orchestra would be accompanying them for the actual performances.

Suzanne tried to focus on her singing, to keep her attention on Jason. Whatever it is, just ignore them, she told herself. But then she looked at Nikki. As soon as Suzanne caught Nikki's eye, she knew what had happened—there was no mistaking that triumphant expression. Nikki was spreading some kind of story about her. Suzanne stumbled on the lyrics and stopped.

"Suzanne!" Mr. Cadenza said. "What happened,

61

my little songbird? Well, never mind—we'll pick it up at the coda." He resumed his abuse of the piano.

Suzanne tried to pick it up, to act as if she didn't care, but her voice wouldn't obey her. It cracked. At first she thought she could sing past it—could get back in control—but then her voice gave out altogether. It was so obvious what was happening in the rest of the auditorium. The way they were all looking at her now was unbearable. And she knew what Nikki had told them, too. Her own sister!

"I'm sorry, Mr. Cadenza," Suzanne gasped, running from the stage.

"Never in all my years of coaching has one of my players ever done anything remotely this sleazy," the coach said, his voice unnaturally calm. "And now I've got *two* of you."

Keith was getting used to feeling like the lowest form of life on earth, but he wasn't sure he was ever going to get used to those killer stares from John. Badillo was looking at him as if he wished he could bash his face in. Keith squirmed uncomfortably on his hard wooden chair in the coach's glass cubicle.

"You let everybody down—me, the team, the school, and the entire town of Hillcrest," the coach continued. "More than that, you let yourselves down. Do you honestly think any college scout is going to take a serious look at either of you now? And you can forget about the pros, Badillo. What were you thinking?"

Keith expected John to respond to that, to defend himself, but he kept silent, his eyes focused on the floor. For the first time since he'd coerced John into helping him, Keith realized it wasn't only his future that had been riding on that game—John's was on the line, too. He'd ruined John's chance at the pros. Keith wanted to say something, to tell the coach it was all his fault, but he couldn't.

"I don't know what you expect me to do about this," the coach went on. "I can tell you that neither one of you is too popular with the rest of the team right now, and I can't blame them. Do you think you deserve to play after this?"

To Keith's surprise, John finally spoke up.

"No, Coach," he said.

"But Coach—" Keith broke in.

"No buts, Stein. Badillo just gave me the only answer a coach could respect. You're both suspended from the team until after the trial next week. And if they find you guilty, you can kiss this game good-bye."

"I feel really bad about this," Keith began, leaning against the football locker next to John's.

It was unbelievable, John thought. After all the damage Keith had done, he still thought he could talk his way out of it. If he weren't Katia's brother . . . John's pulse sped up dangerously.

"I know you're probably pretty mad at me right now," Keith continued conversationally, "but—"

John dropped his battered black gym bag and wheeled on Keith in a fury. Wasn't it bad enough that they'd been suspended from the team and asked to clean out their lockers? Did he have to put up with this idiot, too?

"You don't know squat!" John shouted. "You don't even have a clue, okay?" He picked up his bag and continued stuffing gear into it blindly—cleats, pads, jersey . . .

"I just hope you're not going to hold this against me."

If the whole situation hadn't been so painful, John would have laughed out loud. "You're kidding, right? Or do you honestly think that you're going to waltz away from this? Well, let me tell you something, Keith—if it weren't for your sister, you wouldn't even be able to stand up right now to offer your lame excuses."

"John—"

"Get out of here!" John exploded. "I mean it, Stein. Get out of here before I kick your butt."

Keith finally had the sense to leave.

John resumed his packing. He didn't blame the coach for suspending them, but he still couldn't believe it was happening. Everything he'd worked so hard for—all of it had been thrown away on nothing. I'm just going to grab my stuff and get out of here, he told himself, jamming his practice sweats into the bag. In a couple more moments he was finished. John stood before the empty locker, waiting for . . . he didn't know what. There was something so final about closing it. At last John removed the padlock and put it in his gym bag, but as he went to close the locker door, something caught his eye. It was a Polaroid picture of Katia and him after a football practice—she didn't even know that one of the guys on the team had taken it. Carefully he lifted the tape that held it to the back of the door. Katia—his lucky charm.

Suddenly a single thought became clear to him—there was only one thing he knew for sure. Whatever else happened, whatever else he had lost, he couldn't lose Katia. He stared at the secret picture. No matter what it takes, he swore, I'm going to get her back.

Katia glared toward the center of the crowded cafeteria in the direction of her usual table. On the one hand, she was sorry to be missing her chance to sit with the gang, but on the other, she was never going to speak to Victoria again. Not even if she begged.

"So anyway," her sophomore friend Diane Chapman was saying, "I heard that even her mother doesn't know who her father is."

"How's that possible?" Cindy Thomas challenged. Sometimes Cindy could be really dense.

Of course, they were talking about Suzanne Willis. Everybody was—the rumor was spreading like wildfire. Katia looked across the enormous room to where Suzanne was eating by herself at a table of outsiders. Katia would have hated for someone to be saying things like that about her—especially without any proof!

"But Jeannie Jensen will say anything," Agnes Tu protested. "Remember that time she told everyone that Principal Isaac was a man in drag?"

"I know, but this time it's really true," Diane insisted.

Cindy chimed in again. "Victoria Hill said—"

But Katia had heard enough. Leaving her lunch untouched on the tray, she swung herself up on her crutches. "I've got to go."

Katia didn't know Suzanne that well, but she knew Victoria better than she wanted to. It sickened her to think that all that time Victoria had only pretended to be her friend when what she really wanted was John. Well, she could have him! Katia was through with them both. She made her way to Suzanne's table.

"Hi, Suzanne. Is anybody sitting here?" Katia asked.

Suzanne looked completely surprised. "No, go ahead," she said, indicating the empty seat beside her.

Katia worked her way off her crutches and into the hard plastic chair.

"Look, Suzanne," she said, "I know we don't know each other that well, but I just wanted to say that I don't believe any of it. Victoria's the biggest liar on the face of the earth."

Suzanne smiled, but her eyes were sad, and Katia thought she looked as if she'd been crying. "Well, thanks," Suzanne said, "but it isn't Victoria doing the damage. It's Nikki."

"Nikki?" But before Katia could question her any further, there was a major disruption in the cafeteria.

"Hey, pizza man! Over here!" Pete Brewer yelled.

"Pizza man! Pizza man!" Kids picked up the cry from all over the cafeteria.

"What's going on?" Suzanne asked. "Did someone actually call for a pizza?"

66

Katia shrugged. "Beats me."

The two girls watched with interest as the pizza-delivery guy worked his way through the growing frenzy in the cafeteria.

"Hey, I know him," Katia said suddenly. "That's Jimmy from Pizza Haven. I can't believe someone convinced him to deliver here. And what's he doing with flowers?"

Just as she spoke, Jimmy looked in her direction. Visibly relieved, he made his way toward Katia, a large pizza box in one arm and an even larger bouquet of deep pink roses in the other.

"I finally found you," Jimmy said, setting the pizza down on the table in front of a speechless Katia. "I was starting to think I was going to be attacked!" He looked warily around the cafeteria. "Here. These are for you, too," he added, forcing the enormous bouquet into her hands.

"But I don't understand . . . ," Katia began.

"They're from John Badillo," Jimmy explained. "Look, I really have to get out of here." He hightailed it back the way he had come.

"Wow," Suzanne said. "Pretty spectacular."

Katia felt like dropping the roses on the floor and grinding them to pulp with her good left foot. How dare John pull a stunt like that in front of the entire school? But everyone was staring at her, so instead she barely looked at the flowers and dropped them on the table.

"Open the card," Suzanne urged.

"I'll open it later," Katia said, trying hard to control her temper. Out of the corner of her eye she was now aware of John watching her, waiting to see what she was going to do.

"Well, I hope you're at least going to eat the pizza!"

There was no way to ignore the pizza without making a bigger scene than John already had, Katia realized. Reluctantly she lifted the lid. It was Pizza Haven's special and Katia's favorite: double pepperoni and Italian brown mushrooms.

"Oh, I love pepperoni," Suzanne said enviously.

"Help yourself."

Suzanne hesitated.

"Really," Katia insisted. "I can't possibly eat all this. Please have some. In fact, everybody have some," she said, inviting the rest of the table.

Her invitation was eagerly accepted, and soon everyone around her was devouring pizza.

"Aren't you having any?" Suzanne asked, gesturing to the few remaining slices.

"I'm not hungry," Katia lied. The truth was, she hadn't touched her other lunch, and the smell of her favorite pizza was driving her crazy. But John was watching—she wouldn't give him the satisfaction.

Suzanne looked surprised. Then she followed Katia's glance over to where John had taken a seat alone.

"You should at least take a bite," Suzanne said to Katia in a low voice. "You're going to hurt his feelings."

Katia didn't respond.

"You're going to make him a laughingstock in front of the whole school," Suzanne pointed out.

She was right. One part of Katia would have

liked nothing better. He *should* suffer—he should hurt the way he'd hurt her. But the other part just wanted to get on with her life. She'd had enough public scenes in the last couple of days to last a lifetime. She picked up a slice of pizza and took a bite.

"Good, isn't it?" Suzanne asked, wiping her greasy fingers on her napkin.

Katia nodded as she chewed, but she was practically choking. The familiar taste brought back all sorts of unwelcome memories—memories of John and the times they had spent together. The way he'd introduced her to that very pizza. The way he'd kissed her. For a minute she thought she was actually going to break down and cry right there, but she fought to stay in control. It was sneaky of John to do this to her! She wasn't going to let it work. She finished her slice with grim determination, barely looking up.

The end-of-lunch bell finally rang. Katia immediately struggled up onto her crutches, relieved. Leaving the flowers on the table, she made hasty good-byes and started for class. She hadn't even gotten to the cafeteria door, though, before he'd caught up with her.

"Katia! Wait!" John said.

Katia stopped reluctantly. There were still people all over the place.

"What?" she demanded without turning.

John ran around to face her. "You forgot these," he said, holding out the roses.

It was almost impossible to stand there and face him. He looked so incredibly handsome and

69

sad and sweet, not like the slimeball he really was.

"I can't carry them," she said at last, indicating the crutches with a nod of her head.

He brightened. "Let me carry them for you. I'll walk you to class! Then later—"

"Take a hint, John," Katia interrupted. She tried to move past him, but he wouldn't get out of her way.

"But you liked the pizza, right? I'll send you another one tomorrow."

"Listen, John," Katia snapped. "There was no point in wasting a perfectly good pizza, but don't think it means I want to have anything to do with you. Now, please get out of my way. You're making me late to class."

John stepped aside reluctantly as she started to pass. Suddenly he snatched the card from the forsaken roses and slipped it into the pocket of her jacket. "Just take the card," he urged.

Katia kept walking without a word.

"I won't quit until you smile at me again!" he yelled at her back.

Katia hurried away as fast as she could. Half the cafeteria must have heard him—by the next day the whole school would know they were fighting. She couldn't believe he'd sacrifice his pride like that for her, and the beginnings of tears burned her eyes again.

He has no pride, she reminded herself sternly, thinking of the football game.

It wasn't until she was safely at her desk and her next class had begun that she allowed herself to reach into her pocket and take out the little white card.

Katia, I'm so sorry. Please forgive me. Love, John, it said.

Katia felt something catch and ache on one side of her throat, and a single rebel tear finally slid down her cheek unobserved. Leaving John Badillo was going to be the hardest thing she'd ever done.

Seven

"If we could just narrow down the search area," Ian said, "I think we'd have a better chance." It was Tuesday night, and he and Deb were back in his bedroom, staring at the computer.

"Well, I know I was born somewhere in the East," Deb said. "I mean, I assume I was, since I ended up in Connecticut—it only makes sense."

Ian smiled. "Way to narrow it down, Deb," he teased.

Deb smiled, too. She loved being with Ian. He was so much fun and so easy to get along with.

"Okay," she said, assuming an air of fake authority. "I think we can definitely rule out California. That should make your job easier."

"Thank you very much." Ian laughed. "Seriously, Deb, think! Have your adoptive parents ever mentioned where you were born? Do you have any idea?"

Deb shook her head. "Nope." If only she did!

"Then we're just going to have to guess. We'll do this one state at a time."

He pointed to a well-creased map of the United States that he had pinned to the wall over his computer. "Where do you want to start?" he asked.

Deb stood to inspect the map more closely. How could she choose? Whatever she picked would only be a stab in the dark. Still, they had to start somewhere.

She examined Connecticut. It looked so tiny there on the map, tucked in against an even smaller Rhode Island. She knew that statistically the odds were in favor of her coming from somewhere bigger and more crowded—such as New York. New York would probably be a good place to start. She stretched out her hand and touched New York on the map, but then she hesitated—somehow it didn't feel right. She let her finger drop a fraction of an inch.

"Here," she said at last.

"Philadelphia?" Ian shrugged. "That's as good a place as any, I guess."

He reached for a CD-ROM of all the Yellow Pages listings in the United States—a Christmas gift from his father—and inserted it into the drive.

"I wish I could find my mother with the computer," he said sadly.

Deb couldn't imagine how awful it would be to lose her own mother—her adoptive mother, that was. For all Deb knew, her biological mother might already be dead, just like Ian's.

"I'm sorry," she said, impulsively putting her hand over his on the keyboard.

73

They were sitting so close together that they'd been practically touching for hours, but now they were touching for real. Deb was suddenly acutely aware of how dark the rest of the room had become. It seemed as if there were nothing in the world but her and Ian, sitting in the little pool of light that spilled from the monitor. It was romantic, in a strange way. She felt her heart start to race as she quickly withdrew her hand.

"I'm sorry," she began, confused.

"Don't be sorry," Ian said, turning to look at her, his long lashes emphasized by the shadows in the room.

He was staring right at her, straight into her eyes. But for the first time in her life, Deb didn't look away. She met his gaze, letting herself be sucked in by the intensity of the way he stared at her. He was leaning closer. Suddenly Deb realized what was about to happen—he was going to kiss her! She thought she should close her eyes, but she couldn't. Instead, she leaned closer, too, losing herself in those incredible eyes.

When their lips finally pressed together, it was beyond anything Deb had ever imagined. She couldn't believe the thrill that jolted through her body. Ian put his arms around her and kissed her more urgently, and she responded as well as she could, praying she was doing it right.

But after a minute Ian stopped. "Is something the matter?" he asked gently.

"No!" she said. Oh, no, she *had* done something wrong. "Why do you say that?"

"I don't know," Ian said. "You just don't seem too into it." He let her go.

Deb wished desperately that she knew what to do or say, but instead she sat there and looked at him dumbly.

"What am I *doing?*" he exploded, becoming suddenly angry. "I'm so sorry, Deb. I'm such an idiot! I can't believe I thought—"

"No, Ian." She hurried to stop him. "You—you thought right. It's only that I . . . well, I never kissed anyone before."

"Really?" he asked hopefully.

Deb smiled. "Do you think I'd say something that embarrassing just to make you feel better?"

He laughed, and she felt her pulse quicken again as he reached over and took her hands.

"It's not like I'm the most experienced guy in the world myself," he said. "A couple of summer flings at computer camp—that's it."

"Well, you're two flings ahead of me, then," Deb admitted shyly.

"That's amazing," he said, pulling her close again. "I've wanted to kiss you since the very first second I saw you."

"So what are you waiting for?" Deb whispered, closing her eyes.

Victoria looked disgustedly around the front lawn Wednesday morning as she and Nikki waited for the first bell. School was getting to be more of a drag every day. Even getting up and dressed in the morning was barely worth the effort. No one appreciated her.

Victoria knew she looked especially hot that morning in her new pleated mini and thigh-highs, but what was the point? Sure, half the guys who walked past were drooling over her, but they were all so immature and disgusting. And speaking of disgusting . . .

"I still can't believe what an idiot John made of himself in the cafeteria on Monday," she said to Nikki.

"I thought it was kind of romantic," Nikki said, retying the bow on her blond ponytail.

That figures, Victoria thought. Ever since Nikki had put things on hold with Luke, she was likely to go all mushy at a moment's notice.

"Well, *I* thought it was kind of nauseating," Victoria said, trying to forget how guilty she felt about her part in the whole thing. "John Badillo on his knees to a sophomore! I never thought I'd see the day," she sniffed. "And you know what else? The whole time we were dating, he never brought me flowers—not once."

It sickened her to remember the extravagant display of pink roses that had been wasted two days before.

"I can't believe it," Nikki said suddenly, as if she hadn't heard a single word.

"Are you paying attention to anything I—" Victoria began, but Nikki simply pointed.

It was the final insult. Ian Houghton and Deb Johnson were walking across the lawn toward the front steps, arm in arm.

"Can you believe that?" Victoria demanded. "He wouldn't look at me twice, but he's into that little wallflower! What a loser."

"It is pretty amazing," Nikki agreed.

Both girls stood transfixed as the new couple

crossed the grass, Deb smiling up into the face of the much taller Ian and talking animatedly as they walked. At the base of the stairs they stopped, and Victoria watched in horror as Ian leaned down and kissed Deb in plain sight of everyone. And it wasn't any little peck, either. It was the kind of long, slow, leisurely kiss that made every cell in Victoria's body burn.

"Well, well." Nikki laughed. "I guess he's going to help her find her birth parents after all—and a little more, too."

"Now I've officially seen everything," Victoria fumed.

"Whoa, was that my imagination or did I just see you and Ian Houghton in a major lip lock out by the stairs?" Suzanne asked Deb, adjusting her dark green book bag on her shoulder.

"That could have happened," Deb acknowledged, smiling radiantly as she searched through her locker. "We're kind of a couple now," she added proudly.

"Wow, Deb! That's great. Congrats!" Suzanne said.

"Thanks," Deb said. A total stranger could have seen she was floating up around cloud nine somewhere.

"Aren't you glad I told you to talk to him? You must be so happy!"

"I am," Deb gushed. "Oh, Suzanne, he's the sweetest, nicest guy—I can't believe it. And you'll never guess what else!"

"What?" Suzanne asked, ready to believe anything.

"We found my birth certificate!"

"Already? How?" Was it possible for one person to be this lucky?

"By accident, mostly," Deb admitted. "We started in Philadelphia, and the first hospital we linked up with told us to call the state registrar—and they actually had it. It was like a miracle."

"Oh, Deb, I'm so happy for you. Really."

"Thanks," Deb said, flashing that enormous smile again. Suzanne thought Deb almost looked like a different person—a prettier, more confident person. She had even tied a wide scarlet ribbon into a floppy bow atop her jet black hair—pretty daring for Deb.

"So what happens next?" Suzanne pressed.

"Well, we know my birth mother's name now," Deb said. "It's Jane Benson-Taylor."

"And your father?"

For the first time since Suzanne had seen her that morning, Deb's smile dimmed just a little.

"Listed as unknown," she admitted. "But we're going to start with my mother." She brightened again. "If we can find her, then I know we can find him."

"Sure you can," Suzanne encouraged her.

"Ian and I will go through the residential phone books this afternoon. If anyone can find her, Ian can. . . ." Deb's words trailed off. "But what about *your* father, Suzanne?" she asked suddenly. "Are you going to try to find him, too?"

"I don't know," Suzanne said, wishing she didn't have to lie. "I guess these things take time."

Deb nodded sympathetically. "I know what you mean," she agreed. "It's a major decision."

Suzanne thought about what Deb had said as she walked alone to her first class. What *about* her father? She'd just been getting to know him when Nikki had ruined everything. Suzanne felt herself becoming angry again as she remembered Nikki's threats in the Stewart kitchen. And of course it was Nikki spreading those same ugly rumors about her all over school. Everywhere Suzanne went she could feel the stares, could hear the unguarded whispering behind her back. It was horrible.

If my father knew what his "real" daughter is saying about him, Suzanne thought, I bet things would be different. Well, Nikki wasn't going to win this time, Suzanne promised herself. What Nikki had, Suzanne intended to get: Luke first, then her father.

Victoria pushed listlessly through the floor-length gowns in the designer section of her favorite department store, barely seeing them. After the horrible day she'd had at school, she had thought that spending her father's money on something really unnecessary and ridiculously expensive would cheer her up. But now it all seemed like a waste of time. She moved to a rack of cocktail-length dresses.

Sequined, sheer, backless—what was the difference? She'd never wear it. Except maybe to another of those endless political affairs her father kept dragging her to: the obedient, puppetlike daughter of Hillcrest's up-and-coming deputy-mayor-to-be. The thought sickened her. Her father wouldn't be so smug if the voters of Hillcrest knew his nasty little secret—that he'd run her off the road and left Katia in a coma. But he was so positive he was in the clear now. He and Victoria were the only two people who knew what had happened the night of the car crash, and she'd never hated him more. Blindly Victoria grabbed an armload of dresses and headed for the dressing room.

The first dress she tried on was a knockout— black and cut low in back, with long, narrow sleeves and a neckline that plunged almost to her navel. As far as Victoria could tell, the only thing holding it together was her. The heavily beaded bodice was skintight all the way to her hips, and from there the skirt fell to just above her knees in an artistic drape of clinging chiffon. She twirled to see how it moved. Definite potential, she thought, feeling like herself for the first time in days.

Leaving the dressing room, Victoria sailed back out onto the floor and over to the full-length mirror to get a better look. No doubt about it, the dress was deadly. She had to have it. She was just imagining the black satin pumps she'd buy to go with it when she noticed someone watching her reflection.

Victoria was sure she'd never seen him before. There was no way she'd ever forget a guy that gorgeous. Tall, dark, and handsome, she thought, just the way I like a guy.

"How do I look?" she asked flirtatiously.

"Black is your color," he said, smiling lazily. He had a rich, deep voice that gave her goose bumps.

"It's the only color you've ever seen me in," she pointed out, turning to face him.

"I wouldn't mind seeing you in anything."

Victoria felt her heart jolt. Finally! A guy who understood the game. She arched one eyebrow.

"Black does flatter me," she agreed. She knew perfectly well it made her long, wavy hair look twice as red and her pale skin look twice as creamy. "But then, so does everything I wear." She turned back to the mirror as if she were finished with him.

"Do you have anywhere to go in that dress?" her new interest asked, moving to stand in front of her. Up close Victoria could see that he was older than she was—maybe as old as twenty! Definitely college material.

"What do you think?" she asked, hoping to give the impression that she was breaking at least two hearts a day.

"I think that wherever you were planning to go, I can top it," he answered, very close now.

I'll just bet you can! Victoria thought, but she played it cool. "And you would be . . . ?" she asked.

He smiled and extended his hand. "Randy," he said. "Randy McCormick."

"Victoria Hill," she responded, taking his hand. She had intended to just shake briefly, but Randy held on.

"So, Victoria," he said, pulling her so close that their chests were almost touching. "Are you going to go out with me, or do I have to kill myself?"

"That would be a shame," Victoria murmured, staring directly into his clear amber eyes. This guy was hot! She couldn't remember the last time she'd felt so alive.

"I know a club in New York I think you're going to love," Randy said. "How about tomorrow night?"

"Thursday? That's a school night," Victoria said without thinking. She could have killed herself as soon as it was out of her mouth.

But Randy only smiled. "You go to school at night?" he asked.

"Not exactly," she acknowledged.

"Then it's a date," he said. "I'll pick you up at seven. What's your address?" He took a pen from inside his leather bomber jacket and held it poised expectantly.

Could this guy be more sure of himself? Victoria wondered. But of course she told him anyway, watching to make sure he got it right as he wrote it in ink on his hand.

And then he did absolutely the last thing Victoria expected—he kissed her. Right in the store in front of the saleswomen and everybody. And what a kiss. By the time he let her go, Victoria wasn't sure her knees were going to support her. Here was a guy who knew what he was doing, she told herself. No, here was a *man*.

Victoria watched in a dream as Randy walked away. Just as he was about to disappear from sight, he turned back and smiled—a slow, lazy, suggestive smile that said exactly what she knew he was thinking. And then he was gone. The whole thing had happened in less than five minutes.

"I think I'm in love," she whispered, reaching for a chair.

Eight

"If I win, I'll go free. If I lose . . ." But Keith didn't want to think about what would happen if he lost. He had to win.

Keith knew he should be getting ready to leave for school, but he couldn't tear himself away from the game spread out on his unmade bed. He'd been awake most of the night, playing solitaire alone in his room.

He turned up another card and scanned for a place to put it without really paying attention. Even if he won, his life was practically over.

It was Thursday, and Katia hadn't spoken one word to him since Sunday at the courthouse, not even "Pass the salt" at dinner. John still wanted to kill him, and so did the rest of the team. Going to school was an ordeal—everyone thought he was a traitor, and for some reason people blamed him more than John. Keith had gone overnight from being one of the most popular guys at Hillcrest High to being one of the most hated. No one would even sit at the same lunch table with him! On top of all that, he was grounded until he was sixty-five, and it looked as if his next address was going to be the state penitentiary. He had a lot on his mind.

Keith flipped up another card. "If I win . . ."

Someone pounded on his door.

Great! Keith thought frantically. All I need is for my parents to see me playing cards right now. He was still scrambling to push the jumbled deck under the bedspread when the door flew open.

"Are you going to school today or what?" Katia demanded.

"Katia!" Keith said, surprised. "Hi!"

If his sister started speaking to him again . . .

"I'm not speaking to you," Katia said coldly, reading his mind. "I just want a ride to school."

Well, it was a start.

"Sure. I'm almost ready. Give me a minute to—"

"I'll meet you downstairs," she interrupted, hopping away on her good foot.

Keith hurried to gather his things. This was the first chance anyone had given him since the arrest, and he didn't want to blow it. If Katia would only listen to him, he knew he could explain. He knew she'd forgive him.

He swung his brown leather backpack onto one shoulder and bounded down the stairs, still tucking his burgundy polo shirt into his faded jeans. Katia was waiting by the door.

"Not brushing our hair today, are we?" she asked,

84

looking pointedly at his messy brown curls. Everything about Katia was perfectly neat, as always.

Keith whipped a comb out of his back pocket.

"I'll do it in the car," he promised. "Come on. I thought you were in a hurry."

He tried to take her backpack from her, since she was still on crutches, but she wouldn't let him. Instead he had to settle for holding the door open. She wouldn't accept any help getting into the Corvette, either—she was getting pretty good at maneuvering by herself now—but she did grudgingly allow him to put the crutches into the little space behind the seats for her.

As they drove to school Katia sat in stony silence, her eyes fixed straight ahead. Keith was dying to talk to her, but her expression made it clear that she'd shoot him down if he tried. Still, he had to try. It's not like I've got anything to lose, he reminded himself.

"Katia," he said at last, "I want to tell you how it all happened."

She didn't even blink to indicate she'd heard him. Keith took a deep breath and went on.

"It wasn't like I did it to get rich or anything—I didn't have a choice!"

"That seems to be everyone's favorite excuse," she said sarcastically.

Keith was instantly reminded of John's unsuccessful attempt to convince her of the same thing when she'd confronted him at the courthouse. He knew he was going to have to try a different approach—total honesty.

85

"The thing is, Katia, I was an idiot. I borrowed a ton of money I couldn't pay back, and the guy I owed it to isn't very nice. He told me that I could pay up, or lose the football game, or else. Those were the choices."

"You should have just told Mom and Dad you were in trouble."

"I know that now!" Keith exploded. "You think I don't lie awake at night wishing I had done that?"

Katia turned her head and looked out the window. This didn't seem to be getting him anywhere, Keith realized. With an effort, he forced himself to calm down.

"Katia, look," he said more gently. "This is the biggest mistake I've ever made in my life . . . and I'm sorry. For all of it. But how much longer are you going to treat me like this?"

"I don't know," she said, but then the barrier broke down. "It's your fault that John and I aren't still together!" she accused angrily. "If it weren't for you, he wouldn't even be involved in this."

"And if it weren't for him, I couldn't have done it," Keith countered.

"But you—" Katia began.

"I blackmailed him," Keith admitted. "But the stuff I used to do it with had nothing to do with *me*. John got into that mess with Victoria all by himself."

Katia was silent, but Keith knew the expression on her face—she always made that face when she was trying to be fair, to look at things clearly. Finally he had a chance.

"Katia, I'm sorry," Keith pressed as he pulled

into the school parking lot. "I'm sorry for everything I did, and I'm especially sorry that it ended
up hurting you. Can't you please forgive me?"

For a long moment Katia just sat there, staring
out the window. Keith was beginning to think she
wasn't going to answer him when finally she
smiled—just a little.

"You're my brother," she said. "Of course I forgive you."

John looked nervously around the cafeteria. At
first he was afraid Katia hadn't come, but finally he
spotted her. She was sitting with Suzanne again, at
a table against the wall.

John swung into action. Stepping out a little-
used side door, he ran to the parking lot to meet
the delivery van.

"Okay!" John yelled to the driver as he leaped
the curb. "I'm ready."

The driver looked at him strangely and col-
lected his money. "Here you go, Mac," he said,
handing over his delivery. "I've got to tell you, that's
the most unique sandwich I've ever seen."

"Thanks," John said, not knowing if the driver
was making fun of him and not caring. He lifted
the six-foot-long submarine sandwich carefully,
cradling it on its wooden board. It was surprisingly
heavy and, of course, he hadn't anticipated the
problems he was having seeing over it. Or through
it, rather.

John had had the sandwich decorated with a
dark pink rose stuck through every section instead

of a toothpick—all twenty-four of them. The board around the sandwich was decorated with ferns and baby's breath and more roses, and here and there little bits of greenery stuck up over the edges of the sandwich. Overall, John was pleased with the effect, but it was definitely an armload.

He struggled across the lawn and was all the way back to the cafeteria before he realized he had a big problem. He couldn't open the door again. He could reach the handle from under the sandwich board, but he couldn't pull the door open and walk in—the extra-long sandwich was going to have to go through sideways.

John panicked as he realized the flaw in his plan. He didn't want to go all the way around to the main cafeteria door and fight through the crowds. Instead he kicked at the side door. There had to be someone in there who would hear him and open up. But no one came. He kicked again—harder. Still no one came. The sandwich was turning to lead in his arms, but he didn't want to put it on the ground, where it might get dirty. He kicked again with all his might.

To John's surprise, someone finally pushed the door open, leaving him and his rose-covered sandwich facing a shocked cafeteria. Gathering himself quickly, he edged the sandwich inside and began crossing to Katia. He could hear the girls giggling and the guys making fun of him, but it didn't matter. The only thing that mattered was winning Katia back. He continued resolutely toward her table.

"If she doesn't take you back, come on over here!" a girl yelled suddenly from behind him. Her invitation was immediately met with cheers and laughter from the rest of the crowd.

"No, John. Over here!" another girl called.

"Forget him, Katia!" one of the guys joined in. "Let me have a turn."

And then the whole cafeteria began to chant: "Katia, Katia, Katia . . ." Finally he reached her table.

"This is for you," he said, setting down the sandwich.

She barely looked at him. "Thanks," she said with ice in her voice. "You shouldn't have."

Without waiting to be asked, he grabbed a chair from the next table and pulled it next to hers.

"Look, Katia," he said, not even caring that Suzanne and the rest of the table could hear every word. "You've got to give me a chance. I love you."

"I think you must have me confused with Victoria," she said, pointing. "She's sitting over there."

"I told you that meant nothing," John insisted. "It was all a stupid mistake."

Suddenly he realized that the cafeteria had grown unnaturally quiet. The entire school was listening! Still, he couldn't let himself care—there was too much at stake.

"Please, Katia," he begged. "Just give me a chance."

For a moment John could feel the silence hanging in the air like a living thing. The whole room was waiting to see what she'd say. Would she take him back?

Finally Katia spoke. "You had your chance," she snapped.

"Awwwwwwww," said the let-down students, as if with a single voice.

Disappointment flooded John as Katia looked away. For just a moment he'd thought he'd seen something in her eyes . . . but then she'd shut him out. This isn't over, he vowed, determined.

Luke did his best to concentrate as he stocked the CDs in the front of the store, but his thoughts were on other things. He put a CD in the rack. Nikki, he thought. He stocked another one. Suzanne. It had become a game. Nikki, Suzanne, Nikki, Suzanne, he repeated to himself over and over as he put the CDs in their places.

He just couldn't make up his mind. Nikki had made it clear that she would take him back when he was ready, if that's what he wanted. Nikki. He'd had so many good times with Nikki. She was so beautiful and fun—being with her made him forget all his problems. But he and Nikki were so different. She'd never understand him. The one who really knew him was Suzanne.

Suzanne. Even though he'd known her for a far shorter time, there was already something strong between them. Suzanne didn't make him forget his problems; she understood them—and she helped him understand them, too. There was something about facing things the way they really were that made him feel better. Suzanne made him feel better.

Still, Nikki . . .

"I think you've got enough stock out here now

to last us till Christmas," Rick said, interrupting his mental dilemma.

Luke looked up sheepishly. "Sorry," he said. "It's been kind of slow today."

"Sure has," Rick agreed, looking toward the door as if he hoped to see a flock of customers suddenly coming his way. "Why don't you go straighten up the back room? I'll keep an eye on things out here."

"Sure. No problem," Luke said, grabbing the cardboard boxes he had emptied. He headed for the back.

"Oh, and Luke?" Rick called after him.

"Yeah?"

"Things look really good out here. Thanks."

Luke smiled and continued on his way. He was lucky to have a boss—no, a friend—like Rick. Not only had Rick kept him on the job, but ever since the day after Luke confessed, Rick had treated him as if nothing had happened. No one else at the store even knew.

Luke sighed. Of course, the pay situation had changed. He was eating most nights at his grandmother's now—they were that short of cash. But his grandmother lived in a retirement home and couldn't take them in. If his mom didn't do something soon, they'd be out on the street for sure.

Suzanne, Luke thought again. Suzanne would understand. He'd barely even seen her since the afternoon they'd taken that walk instead of going to the football game, and he missed her. If only he could talk to her at school without Nikki taking it the wrong way! But everything at school was so strange these days—it seemed as if no one was talking to anyone anymore. Nikki and Suzanne were fighting, Keith and John were fighting, Katia and Victoria . . . And Luke had problems of his own. No, it was better to keep a low profile.

Suzanne thought about John Badillo as she rode her bike to Willis Workout on Thursday after school. Strangely enough, she felt sorry for him. After he'd tried so hard, and in front of everybody, Katia had turned him down flat. Who would've guessed he had such a romantic side? He'd sure never shown it to Suzanne when they'd dated. Still, they'd parted friends—or at least not enemies.

Suzanne turned into the parking lot and coasted the rest of the way to the studio. They didn't need her help that day, but there was nothing else to do. She could always take a class or hang around the juice bar for a while. Besides, she was feeling down. Even though Suzanne's mother had lied to her about who her father was, Suzanne was tired of being angry with her. Maybe Suzanne was wrong to hide all of her problems at school from her mother. Maybe she should tell her mom and get everything out in the open.

"Hi, Suzanne," her mom said as Suzanne walked in. Valerie Willis was sitting behind the counter in the lobby, waiting to check in members.

"Hi," Suzanne said, trying to be nice. "What are you doing up here?" Usually her mom had more important things to do than watch the front desk.

"We're not that busy," Ms. Willis explained. "I thought it would be a nice change to sit up here and relax for a while, say hello to the clients, that type of thing."

"You're goofing off?" Suzanne asked, surprised.

"You've got it," her mom joked, leaning back in the chair and smiling.

Suzanne shook her head in disbelief. She couldn't get over the change in her mother since they'd moved to Hillcrest. All of those years her mother had worked until she was exhausted, just to make ends meet, now seemed like a distant nightmare. The fitness studio was doing great, and Valerie could finally relax a little.

And there was Bob Houghton, of course. No doubt he deserved a lot of the credit for the way her mother was glowing these days. Suzanne felt the familiar pang as she wished once again that it was Steven Stewart—her father—that her mother was in love with. Still, she liked to see her mom this way. It was by far the best thing that had come from their move.

"How was school?" her mother asked.

"All right." She was aching to tell her mother how awful it was and all the horrible things that the kids were saying, but how could she now, seeing her mother so happy? Her mom would be devastated if she knew. And not only that, Suzanne realized, but they were talking mostly about her mother. Suzanne could never tell her the ugly things the kids at school were saying about her. Especially since they were so untrue!

"How's Nikki these days?"

"Okay." Suzanne felt the anger rising within her again. Why *wouldn't* Nikki be okay? She still had everything—her family, her friends, her money. Her reputation. No one was going around spreading filthy rumors about Nikki. It made Suzanne sick.

"I just remembered, I was supposed to meet someone after school," Suzanne said suddenly. "I've got to go."

"Who are you meeting?" Her mother sounded curious.

"No one. Just a friend. I might be late for dinner, though," she added as she headed for the door.

"Have fun," Ms. Willis called after her.

But Suzanne didn't need the advice. Having fun was exactly what she intended to do. First she was going home to change into her cute new leggings and a cropped red sweatshirt, then she was going to go find Luke. And once she found him, well . . . watch out, Nikki Stewart!

Nine

Suzanne was just getting ready to leave when Luke came out of the Tunesmith's back room.

"Hi!" she said. "I didn't think you were here."

"Sorry to disappoint you," Luke said, smiling.

Now that she had his attention, Suzanne didn't know how to start. Even in his worn-out jeans and threadbare T-shirt, he looked incredible—even better than she'd remembered.

"So how's it going?" Suzanne asked, picking up a Loving Lobster CD.

Luke shrugged noncommittally. "You know. The same."

Suzanne was pretty sure she did know.

"How's your mom?"

"The same." Luke's intense blue eyes spoke volumes as he tried to keep the disgust from his face.

"Did she find a job yet?" Suzanne asked quietly.

He shook his head.

"I'm sorry."

"Thanks," he said.

He looked away, and Suzanne knew instinctively that he was trying to keep it all in—to keep his feelings from showing. Once again she felt the connection between them. Nikki doesn't understand Luke, Suzanne told herself. If he were my boyfriend, I know I could make him happy—could make us both happy.

Just then Rick walked in their direction. Afraid she was about to get Luke in trouble, Suzanne rushed to make her move.

"I was thinking, if you're getting off soon, maybe we could go up to Pequot," she said hurriedly.

"I'd like to," Luke said, glancing at the clock over the register, "but I don't get off for another two hours. It'll be dark by then."

"Oh," Suzanne said, disappointed.

"Aw, go ahead," Rick said, breaking into the conversation. "There's nothing going on today that I can't handle myself."

"Really?" Luke said, but then he seemed to change his mind. "No, I can't. I need the money. I mean, I need to pay you."

"You'll pay me. I'm not in a hurry. I'll tell you what—if you bring it back by closing, I'll let you use my car."

Luke still hesitated.

"Go on," Rick urged. "I'm kicking you out of here." He smiled at Suzanne. "See that he has some fun for a change."

"I will," Suzanne promised.

"Your boss is so cool," she said as she and Luke let themselves into Rick's classic Mustang.

"Yeah," Luke said, pulling out onto the street. "Sometimes I think he's too cool."

"What do you mean?" asked Suzanne.

"It's just that after everything I did to him, he still treats me like his kid brother or something," Luke explained. "It makes me feel so low. Sometimes I think it would be easier if he hated me—that's what I deserve."

"I see what you mean," Suzanne said slowly. "But if he can forgive you, you ought to be able to forgive yourself."

"It's not that easy," said Luke.

"I know. But look at it this way—" She was about to continue when she was distracted by a movement on the right side of the car.

"Watch out!" she screamed, grabbing for the steering wheel as a little boy on a bike streaked through the stop sign and into the intersection. "Luke, watch out!"

Luke steered the Mustang hard to the left, into the oncoming traffic lane, while the kid on the bike pulled on the hand brakes for all he was worth. Suzanne watched helplessly from the passenger seat as the terrified boy hurtled toward her door. It seemed as if a collision was inevitable, but somehow between Luke's driving and the boy's braking, the bicycle passed miraculously behind the Mustang and safely out of traffic. Concentrating fiercely, Luke fishtailed back into the proper lane, then, shaken, pulled to the curb and parked.

"Wow," he said quietly, running a hand through his hair. "Are you all right?"

"I guess so," Suzanne said shakily. "That was close."

"The stupid kid never even stopped," Luke grumbled, looking back over his shoulder in the direction the boy had gone. "I ought to go after him and—"

"I think he already learned his lesson," Suzanne interrupted.

"Yeah. You're probably right. But man, he scared me half to death." He turned to face her. She was huddled in her seat. "Look at you—you're shaking!" he added, surprised.

It was true. Suzanne was trembling uncontrollably.

"It just shook me up, that's all," she said, but she was afraid she might start crying.

"Suzanne!" Luke soothed, reaching over and putting his hand on her knee. "It's over now—everyone's okay."

She nodded. Once again the electricity between them was overwhelming, blocking out everything else. The boy on the bike was completely forgotten. If only Luke would kiss her!

"You're still shaking," he whispered, leaning closer.

Even though he had almost wrecked a vintage Mustang, Luke was glad that Rick had made him leave work early. Of course he'd wanted to go, but he never would have left on his own. There was no doubt about it, though—being at Pequot State Park with Suzanne was way more exciting than stocking CDs.

She'd been so scared when they'd almost hit that kid on the bike that it was all he could do not to grab her and kiss her right there. The way her leg had trembled under his fingers . . . well, he was trying not to think about it. But following Suzanne through the trees to the river, the late-afternoon sun highlighting her long brown hair, Luke was having a hard time thinking about anything else.

At last they stopped at the riverbank, and he bent and skipped a stone across the rushing water.

"So you've been eating at your grandma's," Suzanne said, reopening a conversation they had started a minute earlier.

"Yeah. I feel bad about mooching off her all the time," Luke said, "but I don't think she minds. She's pretty cool."

"We used to live with my grandparents in Brooklyn," Suzanne volunteered, apparently fully recovered now. She scuffed at the gravel beneath their feet with one black hightop. "I really miss them. I've been thinking about going back to New York to visit—I haven't seen them since we moved here."

"You should go," Luke said, studying her face. She was so beautiful. Like Nikki, only darker— more mysterious.

She shook her head. "I don't know. I guess I just wanted to go back with something to show them—to show everyone. I mean, we moved to this great new place, and my friends were so envious. They're all expecting me to come back and say that everything

99

here is so perfect. I don't want to have to lie to do that. Do you know what I mean?"

"Yeah. I do." It was exactly like the way he always had to lie to Nikki about his life.

Suzanne smiled. "I thought you would. You should come with me. We could go into Manhattan and hang out in Central Park—and I know a great Chinese restaurant downtown we could have lunch at."

"Sounds good," Luke said. Suzanne was standing so close he could smell the clean, fruity scent of her hair. It was driving him crazy, in fact. More than anything, he wanted to take her into his arms and kiss her—just like that time at the golf course. He couldn't let things keep dangling this way; he had to say something.

"Suzanne . . . ," he began, touching her arm.

"Yes?" She was looking directly at him with those deep, searching brown eyes.

She knows! he realized. She knows exactly what I'm feeling, and she feels it, too.

It would be so easy. All he had to do was put his arms around her and kiss her.

But he couldn't. Kissing Suzanne would be the same as kissing his relationship with Nikki goodbye. There would be no going back.

"Nothing," he said at last, turning away. He just wasn't sure he was ready to do that.

"Here's the next one," Ian said, handing Deb a microfiche from where he was standing behind her.

They hadn't been able to find Jane Benson-Taylor on Ian's CD-ROM of residential phone books, but that disk was recent. Now they were in the basement of the Hillcrest library, looking through the microfiche files of old Philadelphia phone books.

"Thanks," Deb said, taking it from him and loading it into the machine. Ian was incredible. If someone had told her a week earlier how infatuated she would be, she would have laughed out loud. But there they were. She stopped what she was doing to turn and smile up at the guy who had already become such an enormous part of her life.

"What are you smiling for?" he asked, smiling back.

"I was just thinking that I'm getting pretty used to having you around," Deb teased.

"Oh, really?" Ian said, pretending to be insulted. "Is that what I am to you? Someone to have around?"

"Of course not. You're also someone to hold the microfiche."

"I am, am I?" Ian leaned down and kissed her upturned lips. "Now get back to work," he ordered.

"Yes, sir!" Deb said with a mock salute. Having a boyfriend was everything she'd dreamed it would be. She'd never been happier.

They'd been going through the phone books for an hour, and they were back almost fifteen years. Deb was sixteen years old. They had to be getting close.

"Give me another one," Deb said, reaching for a film. She took the microfiche Ian handed her and slammed it into the machine like the pro she was becoming, scanning quickly down the names.

"Ian, look!" Deb said excitedly. "Here she is!"

Ian leaned over to read the screen from behind Deb's shoulder. *Benson-Taylor, J., 515 Winter Boulevard,* the listing read.

"That's got to be her," Deb said. "I feel it!"

"Even if it is," Ian cautioned, "do you think she's still there?"

Deb answered with an impatient shake of her head. "She has to be. This is the only number we have."

Ian smiled. "Then let's call her." He reached behind him and fished a roll of quarters from the pocket of his weather-beaten canvas backpack. "There's a pay phone by the bathrooms."

"You think of everything," Deb said, touched.

"I try," he said. "Come on."

Deb was nervous as they walked to the pay phone. This could be it. After all these years, maybe she was finally going to speak to her mother. Her hands shook as she dialed the number and deposited the quarters.

"What's happening?" Ian asked nervously, taking her hand.

"It's ringing."

"Hello?" said a man's voice on the other end. Deb took a deep breath.

"May I speak to Jane Benson-Taylor, please?"

"Who?" the man said rudely.

"Jane Benson-Taylor," Deb repeated. "Isn't this her number?"

"This is a pay phone," the man said.

"A pay phone?" Deb said weakly. "How can that be?" She was so disappointed she felt like crying. Another dead end.

"What do you mean, 'how can that be'?" the man said. "You call a pay phone, you get a pay phone."

"Wait a minute," Ian put in suddenly, squeezing his head in closer to Deb's to share the receiver. "Is the phone in a building at five-fifteen Winter Boulevard?"

"Yeah. So what?"

"Does Jane Benson-Taylor live in the building?" Ian persisted.

"It's a big building," the man said. "What do you think I am, the operator? If you want to give someone the third degree, talk to the landlord."

"The landlord!" Ian said excitedly. "Could you get him for me, please?"

The man hesitated, seemingly unsure.

"Please?" Deb pleaded.

"Oh, all right. I can't believe I'm doing this. . . ." Ian and Deb could hear him muttering to himself as he dropped the phone and shuffled off to get the landlord.

"What a lucky guess!" Ian crowed, evidently pleased with himself.

"Hello?" said an older man who sounded much friendlier than the first.

"Hi!" Deb said, snapping back to attention. "I'm looking for Jane Benson-Taylor. Can you tell me if she lives in the building, please?"

"Jane Benson-Taylor," the old guy repeated slowly, as if he was thinking. "There's no one by that name here."

"She could have lived there a long time ago," Deb said. "Like, maybe fifteen years ago."

"Fifteen years is a long time," the landlord said. "Let me think. . . ."

Deb gripped the phone so hard it hurt. With every fiber of her heart and soul, she prayed for some kind of breakthrough.

"Oh, yeah," he said suddenly. "I think I remember Jane. She went to live with some relatives in New York City a long time ago. Strange girl. Who did you say you were again?"

"I . . . I'm her daughter," Deb admitted. It was the first time she'd said it out loud. "Do you know the names of her relatives in New York?"

But the landlord seemed suddenly uncomfortable. "I can't be giving out stuff like that over the phone," he said. "That's private information. I don't even know who you are."

"I just told you," Deb said. "Please. If you could give me a name . . ."

"If you're really Jane's daughter, you'd know this stuff already," the landlord said. "I've got to go now." He hung up.

"I can't believe it!" Deb wailed as Ian took the receiver from her shaking hands and replaced it on the hook. "We were so close!" She buried her face in Ian's shoulder, a few hot, disappointed tears slipping past her lashes.

"I know," Ian soothed. "But, hey, it's not so bad. At least we know where to look next."

Deb gradually realized the truth of his words. "You're right," she said. "He said she had relatives in New York City. *I* have relatives in New York City."

"So it's back to the phone books, then," Ian said. "Don't give up."

Deb looked up, trying to smile, and Ian smoothed the tears from her cheeks with his fingers. "Do you even know how beautiful you are?" he asked. Then he leaned over and met her lips with his own.

"You look . . . dangerous," Randy murmured, running his hands over the hot, smooth skin of Victoria's bare back. They were swaying on the dance floor, barely pretending to dance.

"You have no idea," Victoria whispered in reply, letting her lips graze gently across his ear.

He held her tighter and kissed her hard, and she kissed him back just as eagerly.

Victoria knew she wasn't supposed to be in this dark, smoky nightclub, but that only made it more exciting. And Randy was right—it was the hottest club she'd ever seen. State-of-the-art lighting effects accompanied the driving dance music of two live bands. They alternated sets from a circular stage that rotated into the wall like a trapdoor, exposing one semicircle at a time. Couples crowded the dance floor, booths, and tables, while the singles hung out beside a long art-deco bar. The smells of beer and perfume, sweat and smoke, melded with the sharp, clean scent of the sawdust being crushed underfoot by the bartenders.

Once again, Victoria congratulated herself on having had the foresight to pick up a fake ID over the summer. In fact, everything had gone so well, it was almost scary.

Her father had already been well into his fifth cocktail by seven o'clock. Victoria had put on a long coat and boots and told him she was on her way to spend the night at Nikki's.

"On a school night?" he had slurred. "What's the big idea?"

"There's a huge test in French tomorrow, Daddy," Victoria said. "If Nikki doesn't help me, I'll probably fail." It was a total lie, of course. Victoria didn't need anyone to help her with her classes, even if there had been a test, which there wasn't.

But he hadn't even argued. "Well, okay, then. Study hard."

She made her escape without seeing her mother.

Once safely in her car, Victoria stripped off the coat she was wearing over her new black dress and traded the boots for the black high heels she had hidden in her leather knapsack with some school clothes. Then she drove the Porsche around the block and parked where she'd told Randy to meet her.

And here she was. It had all been so easy. She sighed contentedly in Randy's arms.

"You like that, do you?" Randy asked between kisses.

Victoria just smiled. No point letting him get too impressed with himself.

"What I'd like is another club soda," she said.

"How about something a little stronger this time?" he suggested, nodding toward the bar.

"I don't drink," Victoria said flatly. "It's personal, so don't ask."

"You're the boss." He led her by the hand to

their tiny corner table, which, miraculously, was still empty.

"Who taught you to be such a gentleman?" Victoria teased as he pulled out her chair. She still couldn't get over how incredible he was—outrageously handsome, fun to be with, a fabulous kisser, and, best of all, not in high school.

"My mother," he said, not in the least embarrassed to admit it. "I'm surprised you never met her."

"So am I," Victoria agreed. It had turned out that Randy's mother had been living in Hillcrest Hollow for the last two years and was even a member of the Hillcrest Country Club. "I probably have and I just didn't know it."

"Probably," Randy said.

"If I'd known about you, I definitely would have paid more attention," Victoria added.

He laughed, satisfied with the compliment. "Well, how could you? She didn't move to Connecticut until after she had me safely locked away at college here in New York."

"Worried about what you'd do to her reputation, no doubt," Victoria said, leaning closer.

"Oh, her reputation is safe," Randy said, looking pointedly at Victoria's perfectly manicured fingers. "It's yours I'd worry about."

Victoria smiled. "My reputation is legendary."

Ten

"Victoria! Tell me you aren't changing clothes in your car," Nikki begged, climbing down from her yellow Jeep. She had just parked next to Victoria's Porsche, and now she bent down to get a better look through her friend's passenger-side window.

Victoria finished pulling on her tight miniskirt in the tiny sports car, then opened the door. "Sorry, Nik, no can do."

"But why are you dressing out here in the school parking lot?" Nikki asked. "Not that anything you do particularly amazes me, but this is weird even for you."

"Thank you very much," Victoria said. She climbed out of the car and began brushing out what was left of her curls from the previous evening.

"No, really, Victoria," Nikki persisted. "What's up?"

"I told you, I went out with Randy last night,"

Victoria said in her most practiced bored voice. "If you must know, I didn't make it home."

"You stayed out with Randy all night!" Nikki was genuinely shocked.

"It seemed smarter than trying to sneak back into the house after I told my father I was spending the night with you."

"With me?"

"Yeah. Oh, by the way, if he asks, we did great on our French test today," Victoria said, touching up her makeup in the Porsche's little round side mirror.

"We don't have a test in French today," Nikki protested.

"Duh," Victoria said, smiling. "Way to catch on."

"Do you mean to tell me that you lied to your father and dragged me into it just so you could go out with some guy you barely know?" Nikki demanded. "Are you insane?"

"Could be. Come on—you're making us late to class." She grabbed her leather knapsack, locked the car, and strode off across the parking lot.

"*I'm* making us late?" Nikki spluttered, running to catch up. She couldn't believe any of it. Victoria had done crazy things before, of course, but this was just plain wild. Out of control. And the way she looked! She was walking as if she'd just conquered the planet. Nikki couldn't help worrying that maybe this time Victoria was in over her head.

"Are you sure you know what you're doing?" Nikki asked. "I mean, I'm really glad you met someone you like, but you don't even know this guy."

Victoria shrugged, all smiles again. "What's to know?" she said. "He's gorgeous, he's got a great body, and he's a terrific kisser. We closed the hottest club I've ever been to in New York, and then he took me out to breakfast. Satisfied?"

Nikki did feel a little relieved. "It's not that I'm checking up on you, Victoria—" she began as they crossed the lawn.

"Not much you aren't!" Victoria interrupted with a laugh. "Look, I'm fine. No, I'm better than fine. Worry about yourself, all right? I see the way you stare at Luke all the time like a hurt little puppy dog."

"I miss him," Nikki admitted.

"But you're not even trying, not even fighting for him. Are you going to let her have him?"

"I don't want him if he doesn't want me," Nikki said miserably. "I just wish he'd want me. And don't even talk to me about *her*."

"About your phony little friend Suzanne? I'm surprised I didn't run into Keanu or any of her other celebrity buddies in 'the city' last night." Victoria's voice dripped sarcasm.

Nikki sighed. "She's driving me crazy. You should see her in rehearsal. She acts like she's the star of a Broadway musical. And even my father wants to know why she isn't coming around anymore. Can you believe it? I asked him since when was he so interested in my social life, and you know what he said?"

"I can't imagine."

"He said, ever since Suzanne saved my life. Even my own father's on her side."

"I warned you," Victoria said smugly.

Nikki groaned. "I know, all right? But even you couldn't have guessed she'd be this bad."

Victoria just raised her eyebrows. "I'll bet Luke's out on the back stairs right about now," she observed.

Nikki knew he was. It took every bit of self-control she had to keep from running right into his arms, but *he* had to come apologize to *her*. If he didn't admit he was wrong, how could she ever trust him again?

"I'm so worried about him," Nikki confided. "The last time I saw him, he made it sound like he and his mom were just one step away from being homeless."

For the first time that morning, Victoria seemed as if she was actually listening. "It can't be that bad."

"I think it *is* that bad. I'm really scared for him."

"Well, why don't you talk to Keith, then?" Victoria suggested. "I'm sure he knows what's going on."

"Great idea," Nikki said thoughtfully. Of course Keith would know. She'd been avoiding him since the breakup primarily because she didn't trust herself around him anymore. The night he'd stopped her from kissing him at the bowling alley . . . well, it was always on her mind. She was afraid of what would happen if Keith thought she was available. But suddenly it all seemed stupid. With the problems he was having, Keith could use a friend, and she could use an ally. "Let's look for him at lunch," she said.

*　　*　　*

111

"So. Don't you like us anymore?"

Keith looked up from his ham and cheese directly into Nikki's pretty blue eyes. She stood before him in the crowded cafeteria with her hands on her hips, a flirtatious mock frown on her lips. She was so beautiful—man, he'd missed her! And there was Victoria, too, looking simultaneously bored and seductive the way only she knew how. When he saw Nikki, Keith felt for a second almost as if the curse had been lifted, but then he remembered everything.

"I thought you two were mad at me," he said, looking down at his sandwich.

"Over a stupid football game?" Victoria said. "Please! Like we care."

"Well, yeah," he said. "And it is kind of my fault that Katia isn't speaking to you," he added apologetically, looking at Victoria.

Victoria bristled, and for a moment Keith thought he'd blown it. "I mean, I didn't tell her anything," he hastened to clarify. "She guessed."

"Well, never mind," Nikki said, sitting down in the empty chair next to him and motioning for Victoria to sit down, too. "She would've found out one way or another."

"Says who?" Victoria protested.

"Come on, Victoria," Nikki said. "Kissing John in Katia's hospital room wasn't exactly discreet. There were only about a hundred people going by there every second. And anyway, you have Randy now."

Victoria smiled—a dreamy, secret smile. "Yes, I do."

Keith was so thrilled to have the two best-looking girls in school talking to him again that he barely cared that he didn't know whom they were talking about. He scanned the crowd in the cafeteria to see if anyone important was noticing whom he was sitting with.

"And Katia will come around eventually," Nikki continued. "Don't you think so, Keith?"

Keith forced his attention back to the conversation. "Huh? Oh, yeah. Sure."

But he wasn't so sure. He had never seen Katia so furious at anyone as she was at Victoria—except for John Badillo, of course.

"I don't know why she's so surprised," Victoria said, crossing those great-looking legs. "Everyone warned her about John."

"I think she's surprised at you," Keith said without thinking. Victoria's cheeks reddened immediately, and her green eyes flashed. What an idiot I am! Keith berated himself as Victoria started to stand.

But luckily Nikki stopped her. "I'm sure Keith didn't mean it like that, Victoria," she said.

Victoria hesitated expectantly.

"No! I didn't!" Keith assured her. "I'm sorry, Victoria. I know it was all Badillo's fault." He knew it wasn't, but he'd have said anything to keep from ruining his chance to make up with Nikki.

Victoria looked somewhat mollified. "Speaking of John," she said, "isn't it time for another one of his stupid stunts?"

She'd barely spoken when a group of students came through the main door of the cafeteria wearing choir robes, Suzanne Willis in the lead.

"What's the choir doing in the cafeteria?" Victoria asked.

"That's not the choir," Nikki responded tersely. "That's the cast from *West Side Story*."

"I thought you were in that play, Nikki," said Keith.

Nikki didn't answer—she just sat there staring daggers at Suzanne.

"She is," Victoria replied. "Which makes this whole thing very suspect."

The group in robes moved to the center of the cafeteria and formed itself into three tight rows behind a single acoustic-guitar player. Then, suddenly, there was John, standing on the table behind the singers, another enormous bouquet of dark pink roses in his arms.

"You'd think he'd try some other kind of flower—" Keith began, but a single look from Victoria stopped him cold.

"May I have everyone's attention, please?" John shouted from his post on the table.

Keith rolled his eyes. John always had everyone's attention.

"Some of you may have heard that the woman I love is a little upset with me these days," John continued.

There was laughter, followed by shouts of "Katia! Katia!" Keith looked around until he spotted his sister blushing at a table with some of her sophomore friends.

"Katia," John said, "this song's for you."

Right on cue, Suzanne and her group launched

into "Leah, Please Forgive Me," a Valhalla song that had been the surprise hit of the summer.

> If I didn't love you so much,
> I guess I might stop trying.
> But if you'd let me do things over,
> I'd wash away this crying.

"You have to admit, Suzanne's a pretty good singer," Keith said.

Victoria kicked him under the table.

"What?" he protested loudly.

> Katia, please forgive me
> For what I put you through.
> I'd crawl on my knees to the ends of the earth
> For another chance with you.

The whole cafeteria was into it now, singing the song that everyone knew by heart.

"I can't believe they changed the words," Victoria complained, clearly disgusted by the substitution of *Katia* for *Leah*.

"Will this never end?" Nikki agreed through gritted teeth.

Obviously there were things going on that Keith didn't understand.

> If you could just forgive me,
> I swear that I'd stay true.
> There's no woman in this whole cold world
> That warms my soul like you.

After a final chorus that rocked the cafeteria, the song came to an end with John joining in on the very last words. "Katia, please forgive me!" he sang, hamming it up. Then he jumped from the table and ran across the room to present his bouquet of roses while the entire cafeteria cheered.

Keith wished he could hear what John and Katia were saying. John was whispering something, and Katia was shaking her head. She still looked mad, and now she was obviously embarrassed as well. Still, Keith knew his sister. Valhalla was her favorite band, and that particular song had been on her CD player so often over the last few days that Keith was hearing it in his sleep.

"If that doesn't do it, nothing will," Keith guessed, his eyes on the arguing couple.

"I would hope so," Victoria huffed.

Suddenly there was another cheer from the crowd. Katia left the cafeteria alone and in a hurry, a rejected John in her wake.

"What's the big deal?" Keith asked, confused. "Why are they cheering?" As far as he could tell, John's efforts had failed again.

"She's taking the roses," Nikki said.

"Suzanne! Wait up!" Luke called, running to catch her.

Suzanne stopped where she was on the walkway leading to the back door of the auditorium. "Hi," she said, smiling. It was amazing to see him, and it was more amazing to see him like this—running after her in front of everyone.

"Where are you going?" Luke fell into step beside her.

She nodded down at her armload of choir robes with an embarrassed glance. "I thought I'd lose the robes before class," she explained. "Not that they aren't the height of fashion, but I'd better get them back in the prop room before Mr. Cadenza finds out."

"Well, that's what I wanted to tell you," Luke said. "I thought it was really nice, what you did for John in the cafeteria just now. I'm not sure he deserves it, but who am I to talk?" He dropped his eyes, and Suzanne knew he was referring to the way he had cheated on Nikki.

"Neither one of us is innocent," she acknowledged. "But Nikki's the one who wanted a war. If she hadn't broken things off, you'd be with *her* right now."

"Do you think so?" he asked softly. "I'm not so sure."

Suzanne heard the hidden message in his words. She turned to face him, and the longing she saw in his eyes made her pulse race faster. The way he was looking at her . . .

"Then maybe I'm wrong," she said hopefully.

"Look, Suzanne," Luke said suddenly. "I was wondering if I could call you sometime—maybe this weekend. It's hard to talk around here." He dismissed the entire school with a wave of one hand.

"Sure," Suzanne said, elated. "Call anytime." She could barely believe it. Was Luke finally finished with Nikki?

He smiled. "Thanks."

They reached the auditorium door, and Suzanne hesitated.

"Well," she said, "I'd better go."

"Yeah." But he didn't leave. Instead he took a step closer—so close they were almost touching.

The pavement where they stood behind the auditorium was practically deserted, and Suzanne ached to reach out for him, to put her arms around him and forget herself in his kisses. But something held her back.

"I guess someday I'm going to have to make up my mind," Luke said quietly.

"Excuse me?"

"Every time I see you, I'm so close."

"What are you talking about?" Suzanne asked, her heart in her throat. If only he would come out and say it!

"Nothing. I'll tell you when I call you." And then he was gone, jogging off in the direction of the gym.

Suzanne put the old choir robes away without really looking. She knew what he was thinking and she knew what he wanted. They were made for each other. How could she get him to admit it?

Lost in thought as she came out of the prop room, Suzanne was greeted by Jeannie Jensen.

"I heard you in the cafeteria," Jeannie gushed. "You sounded great! You should have asked me—I'd have sung with you."

"Thanks," Suzanne said noncommittally, but the oversight had been intentional. She knew Jeannie was spreading Nikki's sick rumors.

"By the way, was that Luke Martinson I saw

118

outside with you just now?" Jeannie asked, clearly trying to be casual.

So that was her game. She was looking for news to report back to Nikki. Well, then, Suzanne would have to give her some.

"Luke?" Suzanne echoed guiltily. "No! I mean, of course not. Why do you ask?" She looked nervously around the empty stage, as if afraid of someone walking in and overhearing.

Jeannie's eyes narrowed, and Suzanne congratulated herself on her acting job.

"I just thought I saw him," Jeannie said.

"Oh, no," Suzanne protested. "What would Luke Martinson possibly want with me?"

"I don't know," Jeannie said slowly. It was clear she was already deciding how best to spread this juicy new bit of gossip.

Suzanne could barely keep from smiling at the idea of using Nikki's own weapon against her. Take that, Nikki Stewart, she thought.

"Randy! It's for you."

The phone clunked down on something hard, and for a minute Victoria wondered what she was doing—she should have waited for him to call her. She looked distractedly around her room, not at all aware of the luxury of her surroundings, before deciding on a seat in front of the antique vanity. Nervously she twisted a long lock of wavy hair around her index finger, watching her reflection in the mirror.

At last Randy came on the line.

"Hello?" said that newly familiar voice—the one that gave her goose bumps.

"Hey," she said. "It's Victoria."

"Victoria! To what do I owe the honor?" It was a strange thing to say. It caught her off guard.

"Some honor," she sniffed. "A phone call. You didn't tell me you were so easily impressed."

"I'm not," Randy said. "Only by you. When can I see you again?"

That was more like it.

"Well, that just depends," Victoria said.

"On what?"

"On where you're taking me."

"I see. So now we're going to play hard to get, are we?" He lowered his voice. "I love that."

"Maybe I'm not playing," Victoria tried to sound offended.

"Oh, you're playing, all right," Randy said. "I knew I wanted to play with you the second I saw you."

Victoria smiled. She was glad she had called after all.

"How about next weekend?" Randy said. "My roommate is going home to visit his family, and I'll be here by myself. You wouldn't want me to spend a weekend all alone, would you?"

"Maybe I would."

"You would?" He sounded crushed—she had him exactly where she wanted him.

Victoria took her time. "I would if it was a weekend all alone with me," she purred.

"In that case," he said, "I don't think I can wait that long."

Eleven

Nikki was early to rehearsal on Monday morning, even though she wasn't particularly looking forward to it. Normally she would have welcomed the chance to sing and act and forget her problems for a while, but having Suzanne playing the lead ruined everything. She was always showing off or doing something like that little stunt she had pulled in the cafeteria on Friday.

Nikki was still steamed about that one. Granted, it was only a partial cast that had sung to Katia, but Nikki was so upset about not even being asked that she'd gone straight home with a stomachache right after lunch. Victoria had come over later and spent the weekend, but all Victoria wanted to talk about was Randy, Randy, Randy. And all Nikki could think about was Luke. It was pathetic—the second-worst weekend of her life. Top honors, of course, going to the previous one, when she and Luke had broken up.

Nikki was still stashing her books unhappily when Jeannie Jensen came in.

"Hi, Nikki," Jeannie sang out, as if they were best friends or something.

Oh, great, Nikki groaned to herself. Just what I need.

Nikki already regretted having said anything to Jeannie about Suzanne—not that Suzanne didn't deserve it. It was just that it *was* a pretty low-down thing to do. Jeannie had spread Nikki's lies so thoroughly that they had already surpassed even Nikki's expectations of damage. The truth was, she was a little ashamed of herself.

"Hi, Jeannie," Nikki said coldly.

But Jeannie plunged ahead without a clue. "I was looking for you Friday. Where'd you go after lunch?"

"Home. I had a stomachache."

"I'll bet," Jeannie said knowingly. "I guess you must be pretty upset about Luke and Suzanne!"

Of course she was, but what did Jeannie know about it?

"I don't know what you mean," Nikki said.

"*You* know. About how they're together now and everything."

"They're not together," Nikki said. She tried to keep her voice calm, but inside everything was in an uproar.

Jeannie put on a look that Nikki recognized as fake shock.

"You don't know! Oh, no. I'm so sorry, Nikki," Jeannie said, falsely sympathetic.

Suddenly Nikki realized what Jeannie was up to. Jeannie knew that Nikki had no idea what she was talking about, and she was enjoying the chance to be the first to tell her.

"I know they're not together," Nikki repeated stubbornly, but she felt as if she was fighting the inevitable. Any second now, Jeannie was going to say the words that would bring Nikki's life crashing down around her ears.

"You poor thing," Jeannie said. She looked around the empty auditorium to make sure they were alone, and then she dropped her bomb. "I saw them together," she whispered.

Nikki didn't ask for details. She was fighting the tears as it was—fighting just to keep breathing. She turned away from Jeannie and started blindly toward the wings. She would *not* let Jeannie see her cry.

But Jeannie wasn't going to give up that easily. Running to catch up, she put her arm around Nikki's rigid shoulders. "If there's anything I can do . . . ," she began.

Nikki spun out of Jeannie's grip and turned to face her furiously. "You can tell everyone you know that Suzanne Willis is a sleaze!" she shouted. "You know how she got Luke? The same way she got John Badillo and any other guy who's ever asked her. Count on it!"

This time the shock on Jeannie's face was real. Nikki slapped a hand over her mouth as she realized what she had done, but it was too late. There was no way to take back what she had said— Jeannie would tell everyone anyway. Nikki felt sick.

It was too much on top of the shock of losing Luke. Who cares about Suzanne? she asked herself savagely. And then the tears came, in deep, angry sobs.

"I can't believe you're on his side," Katia told Suzanne as they walked down the hall after last period Monday. She'd looked for Suzanne at lunch, but she wasn't around.

"I just think you should give him another chance, that's all," Suzanne said. "Aren't you going to your locker?"

"I don't need to," Katia said, indicating her bulging backpack. "I've already got all the books I need for homework."

"How much homework do you have?" Suzanne asked, surprised. "You can't possibly need all those books."

"Well, I don't need *all* of them," Katia admitted. "But it's easier to take them home than to walk all the way to my locker on these crutches."

"I'll help you," Suzanne volunteered immediately. "Here. Let me carry them for you."

"I don't want—"

"It can't be good for you to be carrying around all this extra weight with that bad shoulder," Suzanne insisted.

"It's just as easy to take them in the car," Katia protested. "Keith's driving me home."

But it was no use. Suzanne was already behind her, stripping off her backpack.

"Isn't that better?" she asked. "Now come on, and we'll put them in your locker." She started down the crowded hall without waiting for Katia's response.

Suzanne was acting weird—no doubt about that. Katia rarely even saw Suzanne after school, but that day Suzanne had been waiting for her. And now this strange insistence on going to Katia's locker. Something was up. But Suzanne kept up a running chatter as they walked, and Katia couldn't ask questions without interrupting her. Instead she hobbled along on her crutches, keeping up as best she could.

"Katia! Katia!" She heard the now-familiar chanting from the crowd at the end of the hall before she could see anything. So that's what was going on—Suzanne had set her up for another of John's ridiculous schemes.

"Suzanne!" Katia wailed. "How *could* you? Wasn't embarrassing me in the cafeteria Friday bad enough?"

"Just come and see," Suzanne urged. "I'm telling you—John's like a different person since you broke up with him."

"I'm not going down there," Katia said, turning to leave.

"I think you are . . . that is, if you want to do any homework." Suzanne dangled Katia's backpack in front of her by one strap.

Katia didn't know what to think. A few days earlier, she would have been furious, but now . . . John *did* seem like a different person. She tried to stir up all the anger she'd been feeling against him, but it wouldn't come. All she knew was that she couldn't sleep nights, that every minute they'd been broken up felt more like an hour. She missed him terribly.

"Oh, all right," she snapped, hoping to convey an anger she no longer felt. She resumed her progress toward her locker.

"Katia! Katia!" The cheering crowd divided to let her through. And then she saw it—someone had taped a huge painted banner across all of the lockers in her row.

Katia, I love you. Please give me one more chance. John.

The beginnings of tears pricked her eyes as Katia read the banner. She loved him, too—more than he knew.

"Help me take this down," Katia said to Suzanne, her voice cracking. Several helpful people joined in, and soon the banner had been carefully removed from the lockers and rolled into a tight cylinder. Suzanne handed the roll to Katia as the crowd gradually broke up.

"Since we're here, we might as well put some of those books in your locker," she said.

"You knew all about this," Katia accused, dialing the combination on her lock.

"I helped him tape up the banner," Suzanne admitted. "But I only did it because I really believe he's sorry. Victoria's not right for John, Katia. If she was, they wouldn't have broken up. It's you—you're the one he needs, the one that makes him better than he is. Isn't that what love's all about?"

"I don't know anymore," Katia said, opening the locker.

Inside her locker, things looked different. All of her books and folders were neatly stacked against the back wall, on the inside of the door was a picture of her with John that she'd never seen before, and right in front—tied with a dark pink ribbon—was a little white box sitting on a light pink envelope. She had forgotten that John knew her locker combination.

"I guess I'll let you take it from here." Suzanne set down Katia's backpack. "Good luck!"

But Katia barely heard her or noticed as Suzanne walked away, herding the few remaining onlookers before her. Katia was alone.

With shaking hands, she reached for the envelope and pulled out the card. On the front was a picture of a happy couple on a beach at sunset, and inside was a handwritten message from John.

> *Dear Katia,*
> *Words can't say how sorry I am or how much I miss you. I know what I did was wrong, but you've got to give us a chance. If you can look at the picture in your locker and tell me we weren't happy together, then I'll give up and leave you alone. But I don't think you can do that.*

Katia stopped reading to take a closer look at the photograph. One of the guys on the football team must have taken it after a practice. John's uniform was dirty, but Katia didn't care—she was hugging him with all her strength, her smiling face turned up toward his, their eyes locked in secret understanding. No, of course she couldn't say they hadn't been happy. She turned back to the card.

Either way, I want you to have some-
thing from me. Keep it, whatever happens,
but I hope that someday you'll wear it. You
don't have to say anything—just put this on
and I'll know that you forgive me.

> *With all my love,*
> *John*

Katia opened the little box as if in a dream. Inside, nestled on a bed of pure white cotton, was a necklace of gleaming fourteen-karat white gold in the shape of an open heart. Katia lifted it from the cotton, her eyes fixed on a tiny diamond glittering from the spot where the two halves of the heart curved inward and met in a point. No one had ever given her anything so beautiful—it took her breath away.

Without thinking, she opened the clasp and began to put the delicate chain around her neck, but halfway through the act she stopped. She couldn't wear the necklace. Not yet.

Luke was uneasy as he knocked at Keith's front door. He knew he should have made more of an effort to be there for his old friend, but he had so many things on his mind. Even as he thought it, though, he knew it was a lousy excuse. Maybe Keith wouldn't even want to see him.

"Luke!" Keith said, opening the door. "Man, am I surprised to see you."

"Yeah," Luke acknowledged. "I guess I've been kind of scarce."

But Keith didn't seem upset in the least. In fact, he seemed happy.

"Come on in," he invited, opening the door wider.

"Thanks." Luke stepped in and looked around the empty living room. "Where is everyone?"

"Oh, they're around," Keith said, looking vaguely uneasy. "Doing their thing somewhere. Why don't we go on up to my room?"

As Luke followed Keith up the stairs, he was glad he had come. He wasn't even sure why he'd stayed away so long. It all had something to do with Keith and Nikki being too close, and Keith and John being too mad at each other, but Luke couldn't really say anymore why that should have affected things between him and his best friend. He felt like an idiot.

"Look, Keith," he began as soon as Keith's door was shut, "I just want to say I'm sorry, man. I don't know—"

"*You're* sorry?" Keith interrupted. He looked astonished. "What do you have to be sorry about?"

"I just . . . well . . . I haven't been around much lately. And I should have been."

Keith pushed what looked like three simultaneous games of solitaire across his bedspread and sat down, gesturing Luke into the desk chair.

"Forget it, man," he said, grinning self-consciously. "I wish that were the worst thing *I* had to be sorry for."

"Things are pretty tough, huh?" Luke asked.

"Yeah." Keith looked out a window that was too dark to see through.

129

"You scared?" Luke asked.

"Yeah."

"When's the trial?"

"Friday." Keith began nervously stacking the cards on his bed, sorting them by color.

Luke had never seen his friend so worried. "What can they really do to you?" he asked. "I mean, you're a minor. And besides, it was only a stupid football game."

"I'm afraid it was a little more than that," Keith said, and launched into a full explanation of every detail. "My lawyer is doing what she can, but these guys are out to make an example of me, and Badillo too," he finished up.

"Man, it sounds bad."

"It is," Keith assured him.

"So what are you going to do?"

"The only thing I *can* do," Keith said with a shrug. "Wait."

Luke tried to think of something intelligent to say, but he couldn't. What do you say to a friend who's probably going to jail? Everything he could think of sounded so lame.

"But, hey," Keith said suddenly, "what are we talking about me for? You know, I had lunch with Nikki yesterday."

"Oh, yeah?" Luke said. "How is she?"

Keith looked surprised. "You don't know?"

"She didn't tell you we broke up?"

"No!"

"Aw, come on," Luke said, annoyed by Keith's astonishment. "The whole school knows."

"I've been a little out of it lately," Keith reminded him.

Luke was immediately sorry. Of course, Keith had bigger things to worry about than stupid school gossip.

"Well, we didn't really break up," Luke explained. "I mean, not all the way up. We're just kind of taking a breather until I figure out what I'm doing."

"About what?"

"About everything. You wouldn't believe all the stuff that's going on with my mom. She still isn't looking for a job, and I'm not earning any money."

"You quit your job? I can't believe it."

"I didn't exactly quit," Luke admitted. "It's a long story. But if my mom doesn't get off her butt and come up with the rent by Friday, we'll be moving out this weekend."

"Moving where?"

"See, that's the thing. I don't exactly know."

Keith shook his head with genuine sympathy. "Wow," he said. "I'm sorry."

"There's more," Luke said. It felt good to finally let it out, to get everything off his chest.

"More?" Keith looked like he was ready for anything.

"I think I'm in love with Suzanne Willis."

"*Suzanne?*" Keith's mouth hung slack in disbelief. "But what about Nikki?"

"I still love Nikki, too."

"Oh, man," Keith groaned. "And I thought I had problems."

"Tell me about it," Luke said.

*   *   *

Ian couldn't concentrate as he logged on to the Internet. He and Deb were going to drop in on the Cyberlounge and talk to some of his friends about helping with her search for her birth parents, but his mind wasn't on the project. His mind was on Deb. He glanced at her, sitting beside him at the keyboard, and he felt a familiar thrill as she met his gaze. She used to be shy, but not anymore. Not with him.

"What?" Deb asked softly, smiling.

"Nothing," he said, returning to work.

She put her hand over his on the keyboard, stopping his progress.

"You know, Ian," she said earnestly, "even if this doesn't work out, even if we never find my birth mother, I'm glad I found you."

"Me too," he said, embarrassed. What was happening to him? He used to be the one in charge, the one who would say things like that, but now it was Deb. He wanted so desperately to tell her how much she meant to him, but he was suddenly overcome by shyness. It didn't make sense.

"Not that I think it won't work," Deb added quickly. "It's a great idea to ask your friends in New York to help us out by calling all the Bensons and Taylors in the phone book."

"It would have been a lot of quarters otherwise," Ian acknowledged, smiling. The problem of making so many long-distance calls without getting in trouble was easily solved by the Net. Ian could use the Internet for the same flat rate no matter whom he talked to, and his computer friends in New York City could make the local calls for virtually nothing.

"Okay, we're in," Ian said. "Now, what should we tell them to say?"

"Probably the less, the better. Don't you think? I mean, they should just try to find Jane and then get back to us with her number."

"Sounds like a plan," Ian agreed, beginning to type.

"Oh, Ian! I'm so excited!" Deb exclaimed, leaning over to kiss him on the cheek.

Ian stopped typing. If he couldn't tell Deb how he felt, maybe he could show her instead. He reached for her, and she came to him without reservation, tilting her face up and meeting his lips eagerly. But somehow it wasn't enough anymore, and deep down Ian knew he wasn't going to be completely happy until he told Deb how much he really cared about her. Every time he tried, though, he went into a panic. What if she didn't feel the same way about him? How would he ever find the nerve to ask?

"I have to go. I'm serious this time," Victoria breathed, pushing out of Randy's embrace.

"Just another minute," he murmured, resuming his kisses.

Victoria resisted, then gradually melted back into his arms. It was already two in the morning, so what more did she have to lose? Her parents could only kill her once. She'd told them she was going to Nikki's—now she'd tell them she and Nikki had fallen asleep watching TV. It was a long shot, but maybe they'd buy it. Still, maybe they wouldn't.

"We're steaming up the windows," Victoria protested, rubbing her hand against the inside of the windshield to clear the fog. "It's like the tropics in here."

"Well, you're a very hot girl," Randy teased. "Roll one down a little if you want."

"If I don't, I won't be able to drive back around the block." Victoria lowered the driver's-side window of the Porsche and shivered as the freezing air immediately blasted them from outside.

"Oh! That's cold!" she gasped, glad of Randy's arms around her.

"Roll it back up," he suggested, holding her tighter, "and I'll personally see to it that you get warm all over."

Victoria sighed. Randy was a dream come true, but it was practically impossible to make him listen when he didn't want to.

"I think we should go back to the part where I said, 'Thanks for dinner, it was great, see you this weekend,'" Victoria said, pushing away again—more firmly this time.

"Why would we want to do that when the part that came next was so good?" He planted soft, teasing kisses in a line, working down her neck to her bare shoulder. "Come on, Victoria," he whispered. "Let's go back to my apartment."

"In New York? Now? Are you crazy?"

"Crazy about you," he answered.

Victoria twisted to look out her open car window. The street she had parked on was pitch black, but she could just make out the silhouette of Randy's gold BMW on the other side.

What a night! She'd met him secretly, as before,

and they'd left her car and driven off in his to a fancy seafood restaurant a couple of towns away. It was only supposed to be a quick dinner, but then it became dancing, a couple of games of pool in the bar next to the restaurant, a walk in the moonlight—anything they could think of to prolong the evening. And now neither one of them wanted to say good-bye. Their good-night kiss had ended with him getting into her car and . . . well, it hadn't actually ended yet.

"If my father catches me sneaking in this late, there's going to be a scene like you can't imagine," Victoria told Randy.

Randy laughed. "So you're out a little late. What's the big deal? You make the guy sound like Attila the Hun or something."

"Practically," Victoria agreed. "And he's such a hypocrite! It's funny that you drive a BMW, actually, because I used to, too. If I told you some of the things he's done—and this one thing in particular—you wouldn't even believe me."

"Try me," Randy urged.

But the cold air and a glance at her gold watch—a gift from her father—snapped Victoria to her senses.

"Oh, I intend to," she purred suggestively. "Just not now."

Twelve

"You little liar!" Mr. Hill thundered, blocking Victoria's exit from the house. "I ought to lock you in your room and throw away the key!"

No one had been up when Victoria finally came in the night before, and she had hoped to get off to school that morning unnoticed. Unfortunately, both of her parents were already awake and waiting for her downstairs.

"Now, Allan," Victoria's mother broke in. She was still in her slippers and housecoat, and she looked dazed.

"Now nothing!" he raged. "Do you have any idea how bad this looks? Our daughter sneaking around with strange boys in the middle of the night? What if somebody saw her?"

So that's what this is about, she thought. Daddy and his stupid ambitions. For a minute Victoria had thought he was actually worried about *her*.

"I think you can relax, Daddy," she said with all the sarcasm she could muster. "None of your little cronies saw me."

"Don't you smart-mouth me!" he screamed, the veins standing out in his neck. "I saw you. How could you be so stupid as to think that no one would notice your car just one street over? An hour after you left, I drove right past it!"

"Emergency trip to the liquor store?" Victoria sneered.

"Victoria!" her mother said, shocked.

"It's true and you know it!" Victoria accused, her voice shaking with emotion. "Neither one of you cares about me. All you care about are yourselves and Daddy's being the stupid deputy mayor!"

"Victoria!" her mother said again. She really did look upset this time. But then Mr. Hill moved in, blocking Victoria's view of everything else.

"Now you listen to me, and you listen good," he said in a low, menacing voice.

But Victoria had no intention of listening to him. Why would she want to let him run her life after the pathetic mess he'd made of his own? Even looking at him disgusted her. She turned to walk away, but he grabbed her by the elbow, squeezing it hard.

"You're hurting me," she said through gritted teeth.

"You're going to get up to your room and change into some decent clothes—the way you dress is an embarrassment. And then you're going to go to school and keep your smart mouth shut. If you're not back by four o'clock today, I'll

137

ground you till you're a hundred and five. You got all that?"

Victoria pulled herself free of his grip. "You know what, Daddy?" she spat out. "You're ugly when you're sober."

"Victoria!" She could hear her mother exclaim again as she ran from the room, but Victoria didn't care. Her mother was as bad as her father! Mrs. Hill knew what Victoria's father was—a mean, emotionally abusive drunk—but she never admitted it, even to herself. Mom should do something. She should stand up to him for once instead of always letting him hurt people, Victoria thought angrily.

Victoria was in a rage as she stripped off her crop top and miniskirt and put on a loose flowered dress and leather hiking boots. She was absolutely "decent," but she knew instinctively that the clunky boots were exactly the extra touch that would infuriate her father.

How dare he try to boss her around? She was nothing but a pawn to him—a doll to be dressed up and trotted out at parties. And he was such a phony! If any of his so-called friends knew about his drunken little car accident . . .

Well, he wasn't going to tell her what to do. She was sixteen and she'd do what she wanted, including seeing Randy. The night before, their second date, had been unbelievable. And that reminded her—she couldn't wait for the weekend!

John sat in the bleachers alone. Once the season started, most people lost interest in watching football practice. The cheerleaders were there, of course, working out on the grass on the other side of the field, but he barely noticed them. It was the team he had come to see.

It seemed as if nothing was going right. Katia still wasn't speaking to him, and most of the guys on the team would barely give him the time of day. He tried to keep going, tried to pretend it didn't bother him, but he honestly didn't know how much longer he could keep up the act. If something didn't go his way pretty soon . . . well, he didn't know what he'd do.

And the trial was on Friday. Everyone said John's father was one of the best lawyers around— that if anyone could get him off, it was his dad. Still, lately he had overheard his father saying things that had him worried, such as "plea bargain" and "no contest." Legal jargon aside, John thought that if they didn't find him innocent, any other outcome would still mean he was guilty. And Coach Kostro's words still rang in his ears: "If they find you guilty, you can kiss this game good-bye."

The guys on the field started warming up with a passing drill, running patterns in their gray practice sweats. John *couldn't* give up football—it was the only thing he'd ever wanted to do with his life. Ever since he was little, he'd worked for the day that he would be the starting high-school quarterback. And that was just the beginning; after high school it was supposed to be on to college and then maybe the pros. If he wasn't a football player, what was he? He didn't have a clue.

"Hey, Badillo," Pete Brewer yelled, loosing a lightning-fast pass in John's direction. Even sitting down and being off his guard, John caught the ball easily, naturally. The pebbled leather in his hands felt familiar and comfortable. He stood and returned the throw.

"What are you fooling around with that traitor for?" demanded Kevin Wilcox, running up and shoving Pete. "Come on!"

Pete shrugged apologetically as he ran off after Wilcox, but John didn't blame him. He didn't blame any of them.

Coach Kostro blew the whistle, and the guys gathered around to learn what the next drill would be. There was something about the sound of the coach's shrill whistle cutting through the cold fall afternoon that suddenly gave John goose bumps. He'd thrilled to that sound his entire life. He wasn't ready to give football up—he *wouldn't*. He knew the guys hated him, but he could earn back their respect. He'd play his heart out if they'd give him a chance. He had to find a way to get back on the team. No matter what.

"Suzanne! Over here!" Deb called, waving.

Suzanne smiled as she made her way to Deb and Ian's table at Pizza Haven. Deb was certainly coming out of her shell.

"Hi, guys," Suzanne said as she approached.

Deb stood up. "Suzanne, you know Ian's cousin, Sally, don't you?"

"Sure. Hey, Sally."

"Hey."

Sally Ross was kind of a loudmouth, but as far as Suzanne could tell, she was all right. She wrote for the school paper, the *Chronicle*, and her articles were always hilarious.

"So, how's it going?" Suzanne asked, taking a seat. "Ian, you're surrounded by women," she observed.

Did he actually blush? He turned away before she could be sure.

"I don't mind," he said, smiling at Deb.

He certainly was good-looking. Suzanne hoped Deb appreciated what she had.

"We already ordered the pizza," Deb said. "I knew you wouldn't care what we got as long as it had pepperoni."

"Good thinking." Suzanne smiled.

Deb bubbled on. "You'll never guess what. Ian's friends from the Internet are going to help us find my birth mother!"

Suzanne tried not to raise her eyebrows as she glanced in Sally's direction. She'd thought Deb was trying to keep her search quiet.

"I'm sworn to silence," Sally explained, pretending to zip her lips and throw away the key. What they said about Sally was no exaggeration, Suzanne realized—she didn't miss a thing.

"It's no big deal," Ian explained. "Some of the people I talk to from the Cyberlounge are just making a bunch of calls for us. That's all."

"He's so modest!" Deb said, snuggling closer to him in the booth. "He's actually a genius."

"If you say so." Sally rolled her eyes.

Suzanne had to admit, it was getting pretty

thick. Deb and Ian were obviously head over heels about each other.

"So how are things on the ramp these days, Sally?" Suzanne asked, making conversation. Sally had once spent a day hanging out with the smokers on the ramp as part of a series of articles she'd written about the different cliques at school.

"Not much happening there," Sally said. "Strangely enough, all the juicy stuff seems to be coming from the school musical." She smiled at Suzanne sympathetically. "People are pigs," she added.

"Thanks." Suzanne was surprised but grateful that Sally understood.

"I'll bet you'd like to wring Nikki Stewart's neck."

Suzanne laughed. "That would be a sucker's bet."

"Sally!" Deb protested.

"Chill out, Deb. I know Nikki's your friend. Nothing leaves this table."

Deb looked at Suzanne sheepishly. "It's not that I agree with Nikki," she explained, "it's just that—"

"I understand," Suzanne assured her. "You and Nikki have been friends a long time."

"Yeah. Thanks." Deb turned her attention back to Ian.

"That thing about John Badillo must have been the final insult, though," Sally continued.

"About John?" Suzanne was confused. Was Nikki saying things about her and John now?

"*You* know," Sally said. "About you and him . . ." The expression on Sally's face told Suzanne everything she needed to know.

"What?" Suzanne screamed, leaping out of her seat.

"Jeez! Calm down," Sally said, taking her by the arm and pulling her back onto the bench. The entire restaurant was staring. "I thought you knew."

Suzanne could feel her face flaming a deep, angry red. That was it—the final straw. There was nothing Nikki could do now to make Suzanne ever forgive her. It didn't matter if they were sisters. They were enemies—enemies for life. Suzanne was going to pay Nikki back if it was the last thing she did.

Nikki felt as if she were never going to stop crying again. Jeannie Jensen was an awful person—Nikki wished she'd never met her. But it wasn't really Jeannie's fault, Nikki knew. Sure, she had thoroughly enjoyed wrecking Nikki's life, but it was Luke and Suzanne who'd made it all possible.

It was almost midnight, but Nikki still couldn't sleep. Luke, she thought, the tears falling faster. How could he betray me like this? If he didn't want me anymore, he could at least have told me to my face! Nikki thought, pulling the covers over her head and sobbing into her pillow.

And to lose him to Suzanne was the worst part of all. Ever since the first day of school, Suzanne had been after what Nikki had. Pretending to like her, pretending to be her friend, but all the while working on stealing her boyfriend. And Nikki had trusted her. She writhed at the thought.

A light rap at her door interrupted her sobs. "Nikki? Are you all right in there?"

It was her father, sounding concerned.

She gulped for air, trying to stop the tears. "Fine, Daddy."

"Are you sure?" Mr. Stewart opened the door and stuck his head inside, flipping on the light. "Nikki! What's the matter?"

"Nothing," she began, but it was too late. He was already sitting beside her on the bed.

"Honey, let me help you," he said, putting an arm around her shoulders. "What happened?"

At first she didn't want to tell him—she was still pretty annoyed with him for the way he'd acted with Suzanne. But she took one look at his kind, caring face, and the truth came tumbling out.

"Oh, Daddy!" she cried, abandoning any attempt at indifference. "Luke and I broke up!" She buried her face in her father's shirt and sobbed.

"Nikki, honey," Mr. Stewart soothed, stroking her long blond hair. "I'm sorry. I know how bad you must feel."

Nikki nodded into his chest. She cried and cried until she was all cried out.

"Feeling better?" he asked at last, handing her his handkerchief.

"No," she sniffed.

He smiled. "I didn't think so."

"Oh, Daddy, I love him! How am I ever going to live without him?" Nikki wailed.

"You just will," Mr. Stewart said quietly, turning away. It was strange the way he said it—as if he were talking about something else. But then he seemed to come back to earth.

"If you really love him," he advised, "then you just

keep on loving him. And if he's smart and very lucky, then one day he'll wake up, kick himself in the butt, and come crawling back on his hands and knees."

Nikki giggled in spite of herself. "Do you really think so?" she asked hopefully.

"I know so," her father said. "Personal experience. Now try to get some sleep." He let himself out and closed the door behind him.

But Nikki couldn't sleep. She lay in the dark, trying to imagine her dad crawling back to her mother on his hands and knees. She would never have guessed that anything like that had ever happened, not the way they fought these days. She'd have to ask her mom about it sometime. About when she and Dad had first been in love . . .

Nikki's thoughts drifted back to Luke. Was her father right? Should she just go on loving him and hope he'd come to his senses? It didn't really matter, Nikki realized suddenly. Forgetting Luke would be hopeless. She could never forget her first love—the love of her life.

She lifted the cordless phone from the nightstand and pushed the speed-dial button programmed with Keith Stein's number. It was way too late to be calling, but he had his own phone, and Nikki really needed to talk to someone.

"Hello?" Keith said, his voice groggy. She had woken him up.

"Keith! Hey. It's Nikki," she said quickly. "I hope I didn't wake you."

"What? No! Of course not." Keith was a lousy liar, and Nikki smiled in the darkness. He always went out of his way to make her feel good.

"Sorry to call so late," she said. "I just needed someone to talk to."

"You can call me anytime," he assured her. "What's up?"

Now that it was time to tell him, Nikki wasn't so sure she wanted to. Still, she *had* woken him up practically in the middle of the night.

"Luke and I broke up," she said finally.

"Yeah, I'm sorry. He told me. But it's only temporary, right?"

"It *was* only temporary," Nikki said, her voice beginning to quaver. "Now it's final."

"Say what?" He sounded shocked. "As of when?"

"As of today. I found out he's seeing Suzanne Willis."

There was a long pause on the other end of the line.

Suddenly Nikki felt like a fool. "You already knew about it, didn't you?" she demanded.

"No, I didn't," Keith said. "Because it isn't happening. I don't know who put that in your head, but Luke isn't seeing Suzanne. I mean, he's *seeing* her, of course, but . . . you know what I mean."

"They aren't going out?" She could barely believe it.

"No."

"How do you know?"

There was another long silence.

"Keith!" Nikki prompted.

"I don't know how much I should say, Nikki," Keith said. "I mean, Luke's my best friend. If he found out I was telling you anything he told me in confidence . . ."

"What did he say to you? Tell me everything."

"Nikki!" Keith protested.

"Everything!" she ordered. "Don't leave out one detail."

"I don't think that's such a good idea," Keith said, but she could tell by his voice that he already knew it was hopeless.

"It's a very good idea," she insisted, hope flooding her heart. "Now, start at the beginning."

There was another agonizing silence. "Luke still loves you, Nikki," Keith said at last.

"He does?" She was ecstatic.

"Of course," Keith said. "What do you think?"

"I don't know what to think anymore," Nikki confided. "He's so moody all the time. And I know he likes Suzanne."

Keith's silence confirmed her fears.

"He does like Suzanne, doesn't he?" Nikki persisted. She didn't want to hear the answer, but she had to ask.

"Yeah," Keith admitted. "He does."

"I knew it!" Nikki exclaimed.

"But I think it only happened because there were already so many problems between you and him," Keith hurried to explain. "He doesn't feel like you listen when he tells you things."

"Like what?" Nikki demanded, indignant.

"Like, did you know he might be losing his apartment this Friday, and he and his mom have no place to go?"

"Oh, Keith! That's terrible." Nikki had known things were bad, but for some reason she'd always managed to believe that Luke's problems were somehow exaggerated, that they'd work themselves out.

"Yeah. He asked me if he could borrow the rent money, but I don't even have ten bucks right now."

"I can't believe it," Nikki wailed. "Why didn't he ask *me?* He shouldn't have to be going through this all by himself."

"Well, I think Suzanne's trying to keep his spirits up."

"I'll just bet she is!" Nikki spat. "I'd like to—"

But Keith cut her off. "Nikki, listen. If you still want Luke, you can get him back. But you'd better stop wasting time and start letting him know how you feel."

"What do you mean?"

"I mean, if you're waiting for him to come crawling back on his hands and knees, you can forget it. Luke's got a lot on his mind right now, and you're not the only game in town anymore."

Nikki thought about what Keith had said as she hung up the phone. He's right, she realized. I've been acting like a selfish little girl. She smiled as the beginnings of a plan took shape in her mind. Keith thought she could still get Luke back, and that was exactly what she intended to do.

Thirteen

"Luke! Hey, Luke. Could you come in here a minute?"

Luke groaned internally. The landlord had spotted him cutting through the alley on his way to school.

"Hey," Luke said, stepping into the dingy office. "What's up?" But he knew what was up. The rent was due in two days—or else. And he didn't have it.

"What do you think?" the landlord asked.

"The rent. I know. But we still have two more days," Luke said. He knew he wouldn't have it then, either, but he was desperate.

"Yeah. The rent," the landlord said. "You know, as late as you were paying it this time, I could throw you out anyway. I will if you're ever this late again."

"Excuse me?"

"I don't appreciate getting handed the cash after I already started advertising the apartment," the landlord said. "Tell your mother to get her act together and pay on time next month."

"My mother turned up with the money?" Luke was amazed.

The big man laughed out loud. "Yeah. Right," he said.

Luke knew sarcasm when he heard it. But if it wasn't his mother, then who?

"Are you telling me that someone came over here and paid our rent for us?" Luke asked.

"Yep. Bright and early this morning. Saved your butt, that's for sure."

"I can't believe it!" Luke gasped. It felt as if the weight of the world had suddenly been lifted off his shoulders—as if the jury had inexplicably changed its mind and found him innocent while he was walking down the hall to the electric chair.

"I'll bet you can't," the landlord said, a little more kindly. "Somebody's looking out for you, kid."

"But who?" Luke asked excitedly. "Who did this?"

"Sorry." The landlord shook his head. "I'm not supposed to say."

"But you have to!" Luke protested. "I have to thank them."

"Promised I wouldn't," the landlord said. "Hey, I've got my money. I don't care where it comes from, and neither should you. Maybe you've got one of them secret angels."

A secret angel. It was the type of thing that happened only in the movies. As Luke stepped outside into the cold fall sunshine, everything looked different: the sky was brighter, the leaves were more colorful—even the air smelled better. He walked slowly down the cracked sidewalk, totally aware of his surroundings for the first time in weeks. The pressure was off, at least for a while. He could breathe again. He felt like running, like shouting until he woke the entire neighborhood. He felt like kissing someone.

That was it—he felt like kissing someone. And he knew exactly who, too. She might be an angel, but she was certainly no secret.

"Now I've seen it all," Diane Chapman giggled as she pointed across the packed and noisy cafeteria. "When are you going to cut that poor guy a break?"

Katia followed her friend's pointing finger from their corner table to the main entrance, where John had just made an appearance. He looked as handsome as ever—Katia didn't see anything unusual.

"When I feel like it," she answered. "And what's so funny, anyway?"

She didn't have to wait for the explanation. Just then John turned his back to them to pick up a tray for the lunch line.

"Oh, no," Katia gasped, slapping a hand over her mouth.

John had buzz-cut the lower half of his hair in a straight line from ear to ear. Above that his hair was the usual length, but it was what he had done to the buzz cut! Five block letters had been shaved into the very short dark brown hair: *K A T I A.* They stood out like neon with the untanned skin showing through from underneath.

"I can't believe it," Katia said.

"The guys must be teasing him senseless," Diane agreed, awed. "He really loves you."

Katia reached a hand to her throat, feeling the hard outline of the heart-shaped necklace through the fabric of her blouse. She knew John loved her. All she had to do was pull his gift out into the light, and the fighting would be over. All she had to do was let him see that she had already forgiven him.

But she couldn't. There was something she had to take care of first.

"I just remembered—there's someone I have to talk to before class," Katia said, swinging herself up onto her crutches. "I'll see you later."

"Later," Diane said. She sounded curious but not surprised. Katia's friends were getting used to having strange things happen at lunch.

Katia steeled herself as she made her way across the cafeteria to her old table. She wasn't looking forward to what she was about to do, but it had to be done. There was no way she could ever get back together with John until she was sure about something.

"Hi!" Keith said, rising to pull out a chair as she approached. "Wow, it's starting to feel like old times again." He gestured to Nikki and Victoria, who were already seated.

"Hey, Katia," Nikki said, smiling and looking extremely happy for some reason.

Katia knew how important it was to her brother to have the gang get back together again—and to be included in it—but that wasn't why she had come.

Ignoring the chair and Nikki's friendly greeting, Katia turned to glare at her back-stabbing ex-friend.

"I have something to say to Victoria," she announced.

Victoria looked up, her bored expression studied, as usual, but Katia thought that this time she detected just a trace of guilt on Victoria's perfect features.

"Go ahead," Victoria said.

"Outside," Katia demanded.

"Oh, come on, Katia," Victoria began. "We can all guess what this is about. There's no need to be so dramatic."

"Outside," Katia said louder, her anger rising.

"Fine." Victoria gathered her books and rose from her seat.

Victoria's hair was perfectly styled in tight, shiny ringlets, and her makeup looked like a model's. As she rose, though, Katia was surprised to see that she was wearing a loose flowered dress with an oversized green sweater and hiking boots. It certainly wasn't Victoria's normal revealing attire.

But I'm not here to analyze outfits, Katia reminded herself, shaking it off. "Come on," she told Victoria grimly. She turned and led the way out the side door to the little patch of lawn behind the cafeteria.

Katia was expecting a no-holds-barred fight, and she was ready for it. With an intake of breath, she turned to face Victoria, but Victoria spoke first.

"Look, Katia," she said as soon as Katia turned around, "I know you hate me, and you have every right to. I was totally wrong and I'm sorry."

"What?" Katia was amazed. She had expected to have to force that apology out of Victoria. Victoria's confession left her without an opening line.

"I would have told you so sooner—I wanted to tell you sooner—but I was afraid to," Victoria admitted.

"You were afraid," Katia repeated sarcastically, a bit of the anger creeping back into her voice.

"I know it sounds stupid," Victoria pleaded, "but I really was. I didn't know what you would do—you weren't even speaking to me."

"Can you blame me?" Katia accused.

"No, of course not. It's just that it was all such a mess—such a big mistake. John's apologized and apologized, and look how you're treating him! And for me to do what I did after everything you and I have been through together—the accident . . ."

And then came the most unexpected thing of all: Victoria started to cry. "I'm so sorry," she sobbed, covering her face. "It was all my fault."

"Victoria!" Katia said softly, putting a hand on her friend's shoulder. All of her anger was gone with Victoria's tears.

"No, don't," Victoria said, shrugging Katia's hand away. Katia could see she was fighting for control.

"Don't cry," Katia urged. Suddenly she was overwhelmed by memories of the many times Victoria had said the same thing to her. She recalled how Victoria had comforted her and stood by her through some really tough times—her freshman year when no one noticed her, the accident, Keith and John's arrest—and now she wouldn't even let Katia return the favor.

Katia reached out and gently tugged one of Victoria's red ringlets. "Hey. I'm not mad anymore," she said.

The sobs gradually decreased to sniffles as Victoria wiped at her ruined mascara. "Really?"

"Really."

"It won't ever happen again, you know," Victoria promised.

Katia smiled. "It better not."

But Victoria didn't smile back. In fact, she looked as down as Katia had ever seen her.

"Are you okay?" Katia asked, concerned. "I mean, there isn't anything else the matter, is there?"

"No!" Victoria said immediately. "Nothing." But Katia knew she was lying.

"Are you sure?"

Victoria hesitated. For a minute it seemed as if she was going to open up, but then she shook her head.

"Just the usual at home," Victoria said. "Nothing I can't handle." She pulled herself together and smiled with a visible effort. "So are we friends again or what?"

"I'll get it!" Suzanne yelled, running down the stairs to the front door.

It was just a little game she played with herself these days. Of course, her mother wasn't actually home—she never was—so there was very little danger of them both answering the doorbell.

"Luke!" Suzanne exclaimed, surprised, as she opened the door. But that was as far as she got. Before she could say another word, Luke took her into his arms and kissed her deeply, with all of the pent-up, frustrated emotion they both felt. She slipped her hands under his denim jacket and kissed him back, savoring the sensation as his strong arms closed around her more urgently. When he finally released her, Suzanne was breathless.

"Are you alone?" he whispered.

"Not anymore," she answered, her hands moving up into his hair.

"Suzanne, I meant everything I said to you that night at the golf course. That night I kissed you . . . I've been trying so hard to ignore these feelings, but I just can't fight them anymore."

"I meant it, too," she said, showing how much with her kisses. Finally, after so much time and heartbreak, Luke had chosen her. "But why?" she asked suddenly. "I mean, why now?"

"I just realized how much you've been there for me. And how much it's meant," he answered.

"I'll always be there for you," she promised.

Luke pushed the door shut behind them with his foot, guiding her into the living room without letting her loose.

"I love you, Suzanne," he whispered. They were locked tightly in each other's arms, the lengths of their bodies pressed together.

"I love you, too," she whispered, kissing him with all her heart, forgetting herself in his embrace.

"I just can't believe how terrific you are!" Luke said, pulling back to look at her. "You really didn't have to bail me out like that, you know. It's my responsibility."

"What?" she asked. Bail him out? What was he talking about?

He kissed her some more—soft, teasing kisses fluttering across her cheeks and her closed eyes.

"It's okay," he said. "I just wanted you to know that I'd help you out, too, if you ever needed it."

And then his lips traveled back to her mouth and she didn't care what he was talking about. All she cared about was being with him and the great times they were going to have together.

Suddenly Luke stopped and cocked his head to listen, his body tense.

"What's the matter?" Suzanne asked nervously.

"Shh," he whispered, holding up one finger. "I thought I heard a car."

The sudden slam of a door in the driveway confirmed it. Valerie Willis was home from work.

"It figures," Suzanne groaned. "Come on."

She led Luke quickly into the kitchen, straightening her long hair with her hands as she walked. By the time her mom came in, she and Luke were sitting at the kitchen table, drinking sodas.

"Hey," Suzanne's mom said, dropping her gym bag on the kitchen floor by the telephone. She was wearing an extra-large Willis Workout sweatshirt with black leggings and cross-training shoes. "I didn't know we had company, or I would have dressed up," she joked.

"Mom, this is Luke Martinson." Suzanne silently prayed her mom would be cool and not embarrass her.

"It's nice to meet you, Luke," Ms. Willis said. She crossed to the refrigerator and looked inside.

"Will you be staying for dinner?" she asked.

"I . . . uh . . . ," Luke began, looking to Suzanne for guidance.

"Actually, Mom," Suzanne broke in, "now that you're back, I was wondering if I could use the car. Luke and I were just talking about going out for a pizza. If you want, we can bring some back for you."

Suzanne tried not to flinch under her mother's questioning gaze as she looked back and forth from Luke to Suzanne.

"Or I could come with you and save you the trouble," Ms. Willis suggested.

"No!" Suzanne said quickly. Then, realizing her mistake, "I mean, sure. If you want to."

But her mother just laughed. "That's pretty much what I figured," she said, smiling. "No. You two take the car and have fun. I'll make myself a salad."

They were laughing as they staggered down the driveway in the growing darkness, Suzanne trying to keep Luke from horsing around until they were out of sight of her mom.

"Why didn't you tell her I'm your boyfriend?" Luke asked as Suzanne started her mother's car.

She smiled. Her *boyfriend*.

"I thought I'd save that for the second time she sees you," Suzanne joked, but Luke had grown suddenly serious.

"I wish I could afford to take you somewhere nice for dinner," he said. "You deserve it. If I had money, I'd take you anywhere you wanted to go."

"You know I don't care about stuff like that," she said.

"I know. And it's a good thing you don't, because I don't even have enough money for pizza."

"Neither do I," Suzanne said, smiling. "But I know a little drive-through where they make a great cheap burger."

"You do?" Luke said, catching on.

"Sure do. And I also know a great place to eat them. This really cute guy I know took me there for a picnic once."

"I see." Luke leaned across the emergency brake and began kissing her neck, working his way up to the ear.

"Luke," she whispered, "I can't drive when you do that."

"Then stop driving."

"Don't you want to get some dinner?" she asked.

"Not particularly. Do you?" He was nibbling on her earlobe, sending little shivers up her spine.

"Not particularly," she admitted, turning toward the country club.

She had barely parked the car before she was in his arms again, kissing him hungrily. She had been there with Luke before, of course, but this time everything was different. This time he loved her— they didn't have to hide anymore. For a second an image of Nikki flashed into Suzanne's mind, but there was no regret. Nikki has exactly what she deserves, Suzanne told herself, holding Luke tighter. Nikki would never come between them again.

"Let's get out and check out the stars," Luke suggested.

Soon they were out wandering the close-cropped

greens in the semidarkness. The early evening was icy clear, and they huddled together for warmth, able to talk at last about the things they had secretly felt for so long.

"I'm so glad we're here," Suzanne said, squeezing his hand.

"So am I." Luke smiled.

"Ever since that first night you kissed me . . ."

"I know."

"It was like it had to happen, don't you think?"

"Yeah, I think it did," he agreed, stopping to look into her eyes. "I think it had to happen from the very first second I saw you. It was like we were made for each other."

"Inevitable," Suzanne whispered, just before he kissed her again.

Suddenly she was gripped with a strange panic. "Don't ever leave," she said, searching his face. "I couldn't take losing you twice."

But Luke just smiled.

"Don't worry," he said. "I'm not going anywhere."

Fourteen

I guess she's not coming, John thought. He'd been hoping to see Katia before their first classes started, but it was beginning to look as if she'd gone into the building some other way. Scanning the grounds from where he stood near the back steps, John strained to make out the faces of the people still straggling in from the parking lot. No Katia. And according to his watch, there were only five more minutes before the first bell rang. Just a little longer, he told himself.

The fact was, he couldn't face going to class anyway. It was Thursday, and the trial was the next day. Every time he thought about it, he got this sick, nervous feeling in his stomach, as though he were in an elevator that was dropping too fast. He'd asked to stay home from school, but his father wouldn't hear of it.

"You're in enough trouble already without missing

161

school, too," Mr. Badillo had said. "You made this bed and now you're going to lie in it."

Parents were always so original. There was probably a book or something of clichés they had to memorize before they were allowed to have children.

John's thoughts were suddenly interrupted by the beautiful sight he'd been hoping to see. Katia was coming across the lawn toward the stairs . . . with Victoria! That couldn't be good. John wished for the hundredth time that he'd been smart enough to stay away from Victoria while Katia was in the hospital. He remembered the vicious way Victoria had slapped him after Katia had regained consciousness and he'd made it clear whom he loved. Of course, it hadn't been the first time Victoria had let him have it, and it probably wouldn't be the last. He and Victoria had always been like a match and gasoline—an explosion waiting to happen.

What could those two be talking about? he wondered. He prayed it wasn't him, but he had a sinking feeling it was. It would be just like Victoria to tell Katia some made-up story about how everything that had happened was all his fault. He'd wanted to talk to Katia, but there was no way he was going to beg in front of Victoria—she'd enjoy it too much. He picked up his backpack to leave, but he didn't move.

Katia looked so unbelievably cute that morning. She'd styled her long auburn hair into loose curls cascading down her back, the way he liked it best, and the dress she had on was new and short—he could see the front of it through her open coat. It fit her petite figure so perfectly that he couldn't help wishing he could see the rest of it. Even with her cast and crutches she was adorable. And she was smiling. It had been a long time since John had seen her smile that way. Even Victoria was smiling.

He stood rooted to the spot as Katia and Victoria came closer. They hadn't looked his way—if he kept quiet, they'd probably walk right by without even noticing him. But suddenly *he* noticed something. Something around Katia's neck flashed in the sun, sending out a beam like a lighthouse to a sinking ship. It was his necklace.

"Katia!" he cried, dropping his books. He ran across the grass and swept her completely off her feet—off the crutches and up into his arms. And then he kissed her, kissed her with everything that was in his heart, and she kissed him back.

"John," she murmured, putting her arms around his neck and holding on tight. "I've missed you so much."

"No. *I've* missed *you*," he said, kissing her again.

"Well, that's about all *my* stomach can take," Victoria cut in, dropping Katia's backpack on the grass next to her forgotten crutches. "I'll see you two lovebirds later."

John looked up long enough to catch Victoria's eye—he had to know how things stood with her.

Victoria shrugged. "See ya," she repeated softly, pursing her lips in a mock sulk. He knew what she meant—no hard feelings. It scared him sometimes how they could still read each other's minds with just a glance, but it was also pretty useful.

"See ya," he said, relieved. Then he turned his

attention back to Katia. "I love you," he whispered, unconcerned that they were both going to be late to class.

"I . . . I love you, too," she said shyly, for the very first time.

The warning bell rang, and eventually the tardy bell, but John barely heard them. He and Katia were carried away by their kisses, blind and deaf to the rest of the world. Finally he set her feet back down on the grass, steadying her with his arms around her instead of the crutches.

"Never leave me again," he said urgently.

"Don't give me another reason to," she teased, running her hands through his hair. And then she giggled.

"What?" he asked, smiling uncertainly.

"Your hair," she explained, her fingers tracing the letters in his buzz cut. "I can't believe you did that."

He grimaced. "Neither can my dad. He about had a heart attack, with the trial being tomorrow and everything. Are you going to be there?"

"Of course. Keith is on trial, too, remember?"

"Yeah. I just didn't know if your parents would let—"

"They couldn't keep me away," Katia said almost fiercely. "They've been just awful to Keith. He needs me."

"*I* need you," John reminded her, turning the conversation back to more pleasant subjects.

She smiled. "I need *you*."

"I want us to make a vow," he said, taking both her hands.

"What kind of vow?" She looked suddenly unsure, as if she was afraid of what he would ask.

"It's nothing bad," he reassured her. "Just a promise. A promise that we'll always stay together—no matter what."

Katia smiled. "Don't you think we ought to see how it goes?"

"No!" he said quickly. "I could be going to jail tomorrow, Katia. I love you and I want us always to be together, even if things get bad."

"It just seems like—" she began.

"Promise," he urged, kissing her deeply, blocking out her objections. She responded readily, with more desire than he'd ever felt from her.

"I promise always to be there for you, no matter what," he whispered. "Will you be there for me?"

"I . . ." Her voice faltered.

He kissed her again. He needed to hear her say it.

"I promise," she whispered at last.

"No matter what," he prompted.

She closed her eyes. "No matter what," she promised.

Katia felt like royalty walking into the cafeteria with John at her side—even more so when they received a surprise standing ovation from their fellow students. Her cheeks burned with a mixture of self-consciousness and pride as John led her through the cheering crowd toward their old table, insisting that she lean on him instead of her crutches.

"John!" she whispered urgently. "Hurry up." The

sooner they were sitting down, the sooner people would go back to their lunches and stop making such a scene.

But John was enjoying the attention. "Are you kidding?" He laughed, waving to some of his old football friends. "This is great!"

By the time they finally got to their table in the center of the room, everybody else was already there: Keith, Nikki, Victoria, Deb, and Ian. Practically the whole gang. The only one missing was Luke. And Suzanne, of course, but Katia didn't really expect to see her at any table with Nikki.

"This is outstanding!" Keith exclaimed. "Just like old times." He moved some chairs around, making room on his left.

"Yeah," Katia said, turning to smile at John, but he was busy stealing chairs from the next table so he wouldn't have to sit by Keith. Sitting Katia down on the opposite side of their table, John pulled his chair in tight next to hers.

Katia sighed in spite of her good mood. It was clear that straightening things out between Keith and John was going to take some time.

"Hey, guys," Deb greeted them cheerfully. "Victoria told me you two were back together, but I couldn't believe it."

"Yeah. Congratulations," Ian added.

Katia glowed with happiness as John leaned over and kissed her in front of the whole table.

"Please!" Victoria protested. "I'm eating." She put one hand to her white throat, as if she were choking.

"Cut 'em some slack," Nikki told her, jabbing her friend in the ribs. "I think it's cute."

"You would," Victoria retorted. "Which reminds me, I thought you said we were going to eat with Luke today."

"Where is Luke?" Katia asked, her arms still around John. "I haven't seen him for a couple of days."

"No one has," Victoria said pointedly, looking at Nikki. There was something strange about the way she said it, and Katia thought Nikki's smile dimmed just a little.

"Oh, he's around," Keith said, winking at Nikki. "I'll bet he shows up any minute."

"Right," Nikki echoed, turning on the smile again. "Any minute."

Nikki stood impatiently behind the school, watching the students file out. She could barely wait to see Luke. Ever since Keith had told her that Luke still loved her, that she still had a chance with him, she'd been unbelievably excited.

She couldn't believe how stupid she'd been to break things off with him when she knew that Suzanne was out there just waiting to steal him, but luckily she'd woken up in time. Barely in time, she reminded herself, wincing. She was thankful Keith had told her how close Luke was to choosing between them. But he still hadn't chosen—that was the main thing. Nikki was done playing games and taking chances. Luke was still hers, and she wanted him back. She was going to tell him so the minute she saw him.

But he hadn't been on the back stairs that morning, and he'd been the only one of the old gang who hadn't shown up for lunch. Everyone was coming back together again, just like old times. Even Deb and Ian had come out of the clouds long enough to be sociable, and John and Katia couldn't keep their hands off each other. Sure, John was still pretty frosty to Keith, but it was the first time they'd even sat at the same table since that stupid football game. It was only a matter of time until everything was back to normal.

All that was missing now was her and Luke. Nikki picked at her pink nail polish in nervous anticipation, scanning the after-school crowd. She couldn't wait anymore for Luke to show up—the suspense was killing her.

Leaving the stairs, Nikki went into the main hall. If she hurried, she could probably catch him at his locker. Her steps quickened until she was practically running. She couldn't wait to fling herself into Luke's arms, to kiss away all the bad times, to start over and make everything better.

Nikki turned the last corner and stopped cold, horrified. Luke was at his locker all right, but Suzanne Willis was up against it. She was pinned to the wall with Luke's arms on either side of her, his chest leaning into hers, their mouths locked together in one of the most passionate kisses Nikki had ever seen. Nikki backed away from the scene quickly, instinctively, but they were so into each other they didn't even notice her.

"I can't believe we're finally together," Nikki heard Luke whisper.

Suzanne smiled without opening her eyes. "Finally," she answered, pulling his mouth back down to hers.

Nikki turned blindly away, hurrying down the hall. It was happening again, but this time she knew it was real. She burst through the door and ran across the lawn and parking lot. The tears fell unchecked as she climbed into her Jeep and fumbled with the ignition. The engine finally started, and she pulled into traffic without looking, wanting only to get far away as fast as she could.

She drove through the streets to her house in a fog of tears and self-recrimination. She was so stupid! She'd had everything she'd ever wanted, and she'd thrown it all away. She'd broken up with Luke just because she suspected him of liking Suzanne. Well, she didn't have to suspect anymore—she'd made her own worst nightmare come true.

All Nikki wanted was to get to her room without answering questions. She had to be alone—she needed time to think. But it wasn't that simple. Both of her parents were home from work already, relaxing in the living room.

"Nikki!" her mother said, shocked, as Nikki burst through the front door. "What happened?"

Nikki knew she must look terrible. She'd driven home with the windows open, the tears streaming down her face.

"Nothing," she lied, trying to get past them.

"Is it Luke again, honey?" her father asked. The concern in his voice made her remember the time he'd comforted her before. Great advice he'd given her then—look where it had gotten her!

"This is all your fault!" she screamed, turning on him.

"*My* fault?" her father said, amazed.

Nikki knew she wasn't being fair, but it didn't matter anymore. Nothing mattered anymore.

"Luke's got a new girlfriend—your buddy Suzanne. If you hadn't been so nice to her . . ."

"Now, Nikki," Mr. Stewart began, a little testily. She could see he didn't like the direction in which things were heading.

"You wish *she* were your daughter," Nikki accused wildly, wanting to hurt him. Her father's face turned chalky white.

"Nikki!" her mother scolded. "What in the world are you talking about?"

Nikki didn't know what she was talking about, and she didn't care.

"Just leave me alone!" she sobbed, running from the room.

"Hello?" Victoria said, snatching up the phone quickly.

"Hey there, beautiful," Randy's smooth voice said.

Victoria smiled. The day had been a total waste of time until that moment. If it weren't for Randy, there wouldn't be anything good happening in her life. She took the cordless phone to her bed and stretched out on her stomach.

"What's up?" she asked.

"Just calling about this weekend."

For a second Victoria felt sick—he was calling it

off. But then suddenly she felt the last thing she would have expected: relief.

"If it's not a good time for you . . . ," she began.

Randy laughed. "What are you talking about? It's a perfect time. I can't wait to see you."

"Really?"

"Of course. That's why I'm calling. I was wondering if I could pick you up tomorrow night instead of Saturday. That way we can have two nights together."

"I don't know," Victoria stalled. Randy was the perfect guy for her. So why was she suddenly having second thoughts?

"You won't regret it," Randy promised.

"It might be hard to cover with the parents," she said at last. "My father thinks he's Sherlock Holmes these days."

"What do you mean?"

"He's constantly checking up on me, looking for clues. Heaven knows, he could use one."

"So just tell him the truth." Randy laughed. "That always throws parents for a loop. Tell him you're spending the weekend with me, and he'll be left with nothing to figure out."

Victoria smiled at the mental picture. She could just imagine her mother's shock and her father's outrage. He'd be furious!

"I'll make it so worth your while," Randy promised, dropping his voice to a suggestive whisper.

Victoria rolled into a sitting position and struggled with her shoelaces. One by one, she kicked off her heavy hiking boots in arcs that landed them across the room.

What the heck!

"See ya tomorrow," she said.

"Thanks for dinner, Ian," Deb said. They were standing on the porch outside Ian's front door.

He kissed her lightly. "You're welcome," he said. "Come on up to my room and we'll check my E-mail."

"E-mail. Now *that's* romantic," Deb joked, but she was as eager to see it as he was. If anyone from the Cyberlounge got lucky with their phone calls to Bensons and Taylors, they were supposed to send Ian the phone number by electronic mail—E-mail.

"You know you want to." Ian led the way. "But after that, I'd better take you home. It's after ten."

Deb followed Ian up the now-familiar steps to his room. Everything in her life had changed so much since she'd met him. In minutes Ian was at the computer and logged on, retrieving his messages, but Deb was distracted. For once she didn't feel like looking over his shoulder, watching his every keystroke. She walked around Ian's room, looking at all the things on the walls, his furniture, his overflowing bookshelves—all the things that had become so important to her because they were part of Ian's life.

"Ian?" she asked tentatively.

"Yeah?" He kept his eyes on the screen.

"Stop that a minute," she urged.

He turned from the computer, surprised. "What's up?"

Deb shrugged, suddenly embarrassed. "I just

thought maybe we could talk for a while," she said.

Ian got up from his desk and sat beside her on the bed. "About what?" he asked nervously. "Is something wrong?"

Deb smiled as she looked into his worried green eyes. "It's nothing like that," she assured him. "It's just . . ."

"What?"

How was she ever going to tell him how she felt? She was crazy even to try.

"Never mind," she said, standing up.

But he stopped her, taking her by the hand and pulling her back onto the bed beside him. Suddenly she was reminded of the first time she'd tried to talk to him, at the dance, when she'd lost her nerve. He'd stopped her from walking away that time, too.

"Kiss me," she said, melting into his arms. Their lips met hungrily as they clung to each other. Deb's hands explored his smooth, muscular back, his tense shoulders. He was kissing her more deeply now, his hands on her waist. Deb was losing control, wanting him to be with her forever. Then, suddenly, he stopped.

"I love you," he whispered, looking into her eyes.

"Oh, Ian," she said. They were the words she had wanted so desperately to say. Tears burned her eyelids. "I love you, too."

He took her back into his arms, squeezing her tightly, protectively. "You scared me so badly. I thought you were going to break up with me," he said.

"*What?*" Deb wiped at her eyes. "How come?"

He shrugged, smiling sheepishly. "I don't know.

You wanted to talk. You sounded so serious, I panicked."

Deb laughed, pushing him playfully. "You're crazy. Do you know that? You're the sweetest, smartest, most handsome guy at school. Only *you* would think any normal girl would break up with you."

"Don't say that," Ian said earnestly. "I'm not so great."

Deb snuggled back into his arms. "*I* think you're pretty great," she said, picking up where they'd left off.

It was almost an hour before Deb was aware enough of her surroundings again to notice the clock on Ian's nightstand.

"Oh, no!" she said, jumping up. "Look how late it is! My parents are going to kill me."

"Call them now and tell them I'm bringing you right home."

Deb dialed the phone with shaking hands. Her parents were usually pretty reasonable, but she'd really blown curfew this time. She hoped they weren't too worried.

"Daddy? Hi, it's me."

"Deborah! Where are you? Do you know what time it is?" Her father sounded upset.

"I'm at Ian's. I'm really sorry. We were . . . uh, working on the computer and totally lost track of the time. I'm coming home right now, though."

"Hurry up," Mr. Johnson said sternly, hanging up the phone.

"I have to go," Deb said, but Ian was back at the computer and didn't turn around.

"Did you hear me? I have to go," she repeated. He simply pointed to the monitor.

To: Ian Houghton
ihoughton@alpha.com

Ian,
I think I have your number.
Try 555-9028.
Good luck!

Lucy
lstone@wol.com

It was the last thing Deb was expecting to see. She was still tingling all over from Ian's kisses, and now she was worried about being in trouble at home, too. The sight of what might be her birth mother's telephone number caught her completely by surprise.

"Whoa, this is really happening." She fell back onto the bed.

Ian joined her. "You should call her," he urged.

Deb shook her head. "Not now. It's too late. We'll call her tomorrow—from the library, after school."

Ian nodded agreement.

"Oh, Ian, I'm so scared," Deb said suddenly, taking his hand. "I mean, what if she doesn't want to know me?"

"I know," he said. "I'm scared, too."

Deb looked into Ian's handsome, worried face. For the first time since their search had begun, he wasn't acting completely confident.

And suddenly Deb didn't feel very confident, either. What if her mother *didn't* want to be found? What if she had a new family now and wouldn't admit that she'd ever had Deb? Or, even worse, what if she'd forgotten all about that little baby girl and just plain didn't care? For the first time since Deb had decided to find her birth parents, she was filled with serious misgivings. What if this was all a really bad idea?

Fifteen

John was barely listening to his father as they sat
in the tiny consultation room at the courthouse.
Keith's trial was scheduled to start any minute, and
John couldn't concentrate on anything but his
watch. Mr. Badillo had said they were likely to be
finished by noon, since the evidence was being
heard by a judge and not a jury, but John was full
of misgivings. If only he could talk to Katia!

"Do you understand exactly what you're supposed to say?" Mr. Badillo asked again.

"Yeah, Dad. I've got it," John said distractedly,
his mind on Katia. If only he could see her before
the trial . . .

"Could you pay attention here?" His father was
getting angry. "I've been up around the clock trying
to get you out of this mess. I've had to call in favors
from people I'd rather not even talk to."

"I know."

"I'm saving your butt here," his father reminded him. "With any luck you'll not only be off the hook, but you'll also be eligible for football again. A little appreciation wouldn't be out of line."

John knew his father was right, and he wanted more than anything to get back on the team. But still, he hadn't known he was going to have to do *this*. What was Katia going to think?

"It's just . . . Why didn't you tell me before about making this deal?" John asked.

"I didn't *know* before!" Mr. Badillo exploded. "What's the matter with you? Do you have any idea how serious this is?"

John hung his head. "Yes," he said, ashamed.

"I don't think you do! You've disgraced every member of this family and you're only a heartbeat away from landing in jail. So now you're going to do what I say, you're going to do it to the letter, and you're going to do it with a smile. Understand?"

"Yes, sir," John said. He had no choice.

Katia was nervous. Keith and his lawyer were already sitting at the defendant's table in the front of the courtroom, and the prosecutor was prowling back and forth like a caged tiger waiting to pounce.

Katia knew how afraid her brother was. The night before, after the lawyer had left their house, Keith had actually cried. Now he sat stiffly at the table, looking frozen and pale.

Please, God, Katia prayed silently, I know he's really sorry. Please let him go. But she couldn't concentrate—there was too much noise in the courtroom. Members of the press jammed the back rows, and nearly every other seat was taken as well. Meanwhile Katia's parents continued their running argument at her right, fighting over which of them was to blame for all this. She tried to catch Keith's eye, to wink him encouragement, but his eyes were fixed blindly on the tabletop in front of him.

The back door opened, and more people came in. Katia was surprised but relieved to see John with Mr. Badillo—Keith needed all the support he could get right now. John scanned the crowd, looking for something, and their eyes locked. He immediately hurried in her direction.

He looks worried, Katia thought. She knew his trial was scheduled to start immediately after Keith's. As John hurried toward her in his dark business suit, looking formal and scared, she felt her heart turn over. She loved him so much—what if he and Keith both went to jail?

John knelt quickly in the aisle at her side and lightly touched the open heart around her neck.

"Just remember that whatever happens here today, I love you," he said urgently. "I don't have a choice about this."

"A choice about what?" Katia asked, confused. "What are you talking about?"

But just then the bailiff at the front of the room called for order. John's father pulled John up by the elbow and hustled him off to two seats near the front as the judge swept in and took the bench. Katia's eyes followed John's back. The buzz cut had been shaved, just as he'd warned her, and the rest of his hair had been cut so short to offset the shaved portion that it almost looked as if he'd joined the military. He sat down and glanced nervously back over his shoulder.

"I love you," he mouthed silently, but before she could respond, his father made him face the front.

The case against Keith began abruptly, with a lot of legal gibberish that Katia didn't understand. Then the charges were read, and Keith was accused of racketeering. Katia knew by now that racketeering meant participating in an illegal organized activity—gambling, in Keith's case.

Keith had pleaded not guilty at his arraignment, his lawyer arguing that Keith wasn't part of the organized racket and that he'd been coerced into participating. But that day she was going to have to convince the judge, and there was only one way to do that—Keith was going to have to tell the court about Tony the bookie, his "loans," and his threats. If Keith could make the judge understand, maybe she'd go easy on him, and on John too. But Tony had made it crystal clear what he'd do to Keith if he opened his mouth.

Keith looked terrified, and Katia felt sick.

The prosecutor walked smugly onto the floor before the judge. "If it please the court," he said, "the State calls its first witness in the case of the People vs. Keith Stein—Mr. John Badillo."

Katia gasped as John rose and made his way unsteadily to the witness stand.

"Do you swear to tell the truth, the whole truth, and nothing but the truth, so help you God?" the bailiff asked him.

"I do." John sat down heavily in the enormous chair.

The prosecutor took the floor again. "As Your Honor knows, Mr. Badillo was to be tried on similar charges this afternoon. However, the State has agreed to drop its case against Mr. Badillo in exchange for his testimony here against Mr. Stein."

The courtroom erupted with surprised exclamations from the onlookers while the judge banged her gavel in an attempt to restore order. Katia watched in a nightmare as her brother's face gradually changed from shocked to panicky to furious. It couldn't be true! She looked hopefully from Keith to John, but John wouldn't meet her eyes.

"Is that correct, Mr. Badillo?" the judge asked.

Katia held her breath.

"Yes, Your Honor," John said.

Katia's shocked cry pierced the courtroom. How could John betray her like this, after everything he'd said about loving her? She fumbled for her crutches and swung herself onto her feet, only dimly aware she was creating a scene. The camera flashes popped everywhere and the gavel pounded emphatically as Katia stumbled blindly up the aisle and out into the hall.

Victoria surveyed herself in her bedroom mirror with satisfaction. She looked perfect. Her ultrashort, ultra-skintight new black miniskirt showed every curve and went just right with her sheer black stockings and black pumps with three-inch heels. It hadn't been easy to find a top that could carry off the skirt, but in the end Victoria had succeeded with a fluffy black angora sweater. She smiled as she pictured the way she'd have Randy eating out of her hand.

Hurriedly she fluffed her hair and applied a final coat of lipstick. She had decided to leave without telling her parents where she was going, and she wanted to get out of the house before they showed up. She grabbed her weekend bag and was almost to the front door when her father stopped her.

"Where do you think you're going?" he barked, coming out of the den.

When did he get home? Victoria wondered frantically. She braced herself for the battle.

"To see a friend," she said, looking past him to the door.

"Not dressed like that, you're not," Mr. Hill said, coming closer. "You look indecent."

"What do you know about decency?" Victoria countered.

"And what's with the suitcase? You're not leaving this house," her father sneered, blocking the door.

"I am too," Victoria said, furious. "I'm sick of your telling me what to do. For your information, I'm going to New York to spend the weekend with Randy."

Mr. Hill raised his hand menacingly. "You can't honestly think I'd let you go to New York City to play house with your little boyfriend. You're not taking a single step anywhere."

"Don't you threaten me!" Victoria yelled. Everything she'd been keeping inside for so long suddenly flashed to the surface, out of control.

"I'm going! Or do you want the voters of Hillcrest to find out who was responsible for the terrible car accident that left Katia in a coma?"

Mr. Hill blanched, stunned, but immediately regained control of himself.

"You wouldn't dare," he said. "And if you did, I'd—"

"But it would be too late, wouldn't it, Daddy?" Victoria interrupted. "Nothing you could do to me then could save your precious reputation."

Her father faltered. "You haven't got the guts," he spat.

"Try me," Victoria dared him.

They stood there glaring at each other for what felt like hours, each of them waiting for the other to back down. But Victoria held her ground.

"Fine. Go," Mr. Hill said at last. "Why should I care what you do with yourself?"

"You disgust me, Daddy." Victoria pushed past him out the door. She was halfway down the walkway before he called out after her.

"And what am I supposed to tell your mother?" he demanded.

"Tell her whatever you want," Victoria shot back over her shoulder. "But tell her I had your permission."

The door slammed angrily behind her, and as she sailed triumphantly down the driveway to Randy's waiting car, Victoria felt like a new woman. Things around the Hill residence were going to be a lot different from now on.

*　　　*　　　*

"Here goes nothing," Deb said nervously, dropping her quarters into the slot in the library pay phone. "It's ringing," she whispered to Ian.

"Hello?" said a woman's voice, answering almost immediately.

"Is this Jane Benson-Taylor?" Deb asked, her heart pounding.

"This is Jane Benson. Who is this?"

"My name is Deb—uh, Deborah Johnson. I'm looking for Jane Benson-Taylor. Is she there, please?"

"Janie doesn't live here anymore," the woman said. "How did you get this number?"

"Uh, from a friend," Deb improvised. "But you do know Jane, right?"

"I'm her aunt."

Deb looked at Ian excitedly, and he smiled his encouragement.

"Could you tell me where she is, please?" Deb asked. "I really need to talk to her."

"Poor Janie," the woman said, not answering Deb's question.

"Poor?" Deb repeated, her pulse racing. "Why poor?"

But Jane Benson was suddenly on her guard. "Who did you say you were again?" she asked sharply.

"My name's Deb Johnson. I'm—Jane's daughter."

"I'm hanging up," Ms. Benson snapped. "Janie doesn't have a daughter."

"No! Please!" Deb begged. "She does!"

184

"She doesn't. Except . . ." The aunt's words trailed off, and she seemed suddenly uncertain. "You're not the little girl, are you? The one she gave up?"

"Yes! That's me," Deb said joyfully. "Please, you have to tell me where she is."

There was a long pause, then at last Jane Benson spoke. "Honey, it's best you just go on with your life and forget about Janie," she said, not unkindly.

"Is she dead?" Deb asked unsteadily. Ian squeezed her hand in immediate sympathy.

"No. No, she's not."

"Then what?" She was sick with suspense.

"The last I heard," Ms. Benson began, "she was upstate in the hospital they have there. Then, well, she got out, and we don't really know where she is."

Deb didn't understand. Her mother was sick? How could someone just leave the hospital without anyone knowing? It didn't make sense.

"What hospital?" Deb asked. "What do you mean?"

And then came the frightening answer: "Child, your mother is stark raving mad!"

About the Author

Jennifer Baker is the author of two dozen young adult and middle grade novels. She is also the producer for TV Guide Online's teen area and teaches creative writing workshops for elementary and junior high school students. She lives in New York City with her husband and son.

For everyone who believes— a romantic and suspenseful new trilogy

by Elizabeth Chandler

When Ivy loses her boyfriend, Tristan, in a car accident, she also loses her faith in angels. But Tristan is now an angel himself, desperately trying to protect Ivy. Only the power of love can save her...and set her free to love again.

Volume I
Kissed by an Angel

Volume II
The Power of Love

Volume III
Soulmates

Available from Archway Paperbacks
Published by Pocket Books   1110-01

Printed in the United States
By Bookmasters